THE SHERIFF MEETS HIS MATCH

by

Jacquie Biggar

ISBN No. 978-1-988126-00-5

Please Note

Cover Design and Interior format by The Killion Group

http://thekilliongroupinc.com

DEDICATION

I have so many people I'd like to thank. First, and foremost my husband, Robert John. Without you I wouldn't have had the courage to pursue my dreams, thank you.

My mom, who has always been my guiding light and allows me to toss ideas with her. Thank you.

To my daughter, Brandy, my inspiration to never give up.

To my critique buddies, you know who you are. Without you pushing me to better myself, this book might never have happened.

To my beta readers for their tremendous input and the reviewers who are key to a writer's success. Thank you.

And last but not least, to Kim Killion and Jennifer Jakes, for the beautiful cover I'm so proud of and the formatting and uploading services you provide. Thank you.

"Jack." She inhaled, panting like she'd just run the Boston marathon. "Jack, we have to stop."

"Hmm?" he hummed and the vibration tickled her core and made her ache with needs and desires fated to be unfulfilled.

"My uncle is in the other room."

That got a reaction, but not the one she expected.

Instead of leaping away like a scalded cat, Jack laid his forehead alongside hers and took a few cleansing breaths before leaning back.

"You don't know how relieved I am to hear that." And then he saw her puzzled frown. "I heard a male voice when I arrived and assumed you had a man here."

As if that should explain everything.

Laurel scowled. "I do have a man here. I just told you that."

Now he was getting irritated also. He stood straight and glared into her upturned face. "Don't be an idiot," he said.

She gasped in outrage.

"I was talking about a lover, of course," he growled.

What the h-e-double-l did that mean, *of course*?

Men.

You can't live with them, and you can't shoot 'em. It's a felony.

CHAPTER ONE

Jack Garrett sat in his cruiser hidden behind the updated *Welcome to Tidal Falls, Washington* sign, *population eight thousand and one.* The, *and one* being his Aunt Tess's newest godson, Caleb. She liked to claim that without her help, Nick Kelley and Sara Reed might never have fallen in love and given birth to their little boy.

He chewed on his donut, wiped the crumbs from his shirt, and thanked Christ they hadn't set their matchmaking eyes on him.

Yet.

Tess, along with his friend Jared's mom, Grace, and her housemate Susan, considered it their life's work to entrap every unsuspecting bachelor that dared set foot anywhere within their radar. The three women took pride in their so-called ability to find true love.

Love. Jack almost choked on his lukewarm coffee. He had serious doubts such an animal truly existed. It certainly hadn't in his case. Even his brother Ty had only recently found his mate, Katy Fowler, after a ten-year separation and a near death experience. If that's what it took to have a warm body in his bed, he'd pass.

Snow began to accumulate on the windshield so Jack cranked the key and started up the wipers. Winter was making an early appearance this year and causing him no end of grief. It was amazing how stupid drivers could be under adverse road conditions. Seemed like the worse the weather; the faster they had to fly, and sometimes it came at the cost of lives. He'd lost count of how many callouts he'd been on this month, and it was only the middle of November. If the temperature would cooperate and drop a few degrees it could do a world of good. Instead, it hovered around the freezing mark which was just warm enough to make the roads shitty.

He lifted his coffee to his lips and swore when a little blue pisspot flew by him on the road, a puffy cloud of loose snow causing a temporary whiteout behind its skidding tires.

Jack had the cup in the holder and the car in gear almost before the snow settled. His foot punched the gas while the hand not holding onto the wheel reached over and flicked on the sirens. His car did a little fishtail as it hit the pavement from the gravel verge but he got it under control quickly enough. Winter tires made a big difference, too bad no one told that to the driver of the car in front of him. It was swerving all over the place. He wasn't sure how the shit-for-brains driving kept the vehicle on the road. Good thing most people were smart enough to stay indoors during a storm and the highway was relatively quiet.

It took longer than it should have for whoever it was to notice his lights. Finally brake lights flashed and the car inched over to the shoulder. At least they were smart enough not to pump the brakes.

Jack stayed on their tail until they stopped and then he parked behind them, half on, half off the road. It would be just his luck to pull someone over for a traffic violation and end up getting run down. His daughter would really be pissed off then. The thought of his teenager left alone in the world because of some idiot's careless driving did nothing to ease his temper. This guy was going to get an earful.

He took his time and set up his computer to run the database of license plates, though the one on the car in front of him was almost too snow-encrusted to read. While waiting, he grabbed his leather gloves from the seat beside him and stepped out of the car.

A blast of what felt like a Canadian wind had him hurrying to zip closed his shearling jacket and pull the collar up to protect his neck. He trudged through the drifting snow toward the driver's side window of the speed freak, careful to keep behind the line of his cruiser in case any other idiots were on the road today. The glass was so frosty he couldn't see the person on the other side. The tires weren't the only problem with the car, the heater didn't work either.

Jack waited, but when the occupant made no effort to roll down their window he impatiently pounded on the glass with a closed fist. A little shriek came from inside. The door creaked open and he backed out of the way, his hand on the butt of his gun. You couldn't be too careful these days, even if this was a normally quiet little town.

A shapely calf encased in black leather boots with killer heels swung over the door-jam and set down gingerly into the snow. Jack's stunned gaze followed the length of nylon-clad leg up to a thigh-hugging black skirt and a fuzzy, fur jacket in bright pink. Who the heck wore furs anymore? Curious, he lifted his eyes and met the honey brown gaze of his new secretary, Laurel Thomas.

Why was he even surprised?

"Miss Thomas."

Jack crossed his arms and rocked back on the much shorter heels of his cowboy boots. "Do you realize we're in the middle of a snowstorm? Where are you going in such an all-fired hurry you'd risk your life to get there?" And where did she get the car? So far as he knew, she'd always walked to the office from wherever she was staying.

She glared at him before stepping out of the car, only to gasp when her foot slid out from under her and she almost went down. Jack reached out and grabbed her arm to hold her upright, contrarily wishing he'd forgotten his gloves. Bet that fur was soft. It looked real soft against the blush of her cheeks.

Frowning, he released her as soon as he was sure she wasn't going to land on her… assets. Her nose was pink. It was kinda cute actually. What was he thinking? There was nothing *cute* about this situation. She could have been seriously injured, or hurt someone else with her carelessness. He was tempted to throw the book at her—that is until he looked into those golden brown depths and saw a hint of fear she couldn't quite hide.

What the hell?

Was she afraid of him? No, her attention was on the road she'd just traveled. He glanced over his shoulder, but there was nothing except swirling clouds of powdery white snow and a howling northern wind. If this kept up ol' Hank was going to have a busy night on the plow truck.

"Why did you pull me over?"

The haughty voice tugged his head around in disbelief. Was she kidding? Her chin tipped up in a defiant gesture and she crossed her arms under her healthy chest—not that he was looking.

"I'm asking the questions, *Miss Thomas*." What was it about this woman that made him feel like a cat getting rubbed the wrong way? Twitchy.

~~~*~~~

Laurel couldn't believe her luck. Nothing had gone right for her in more months than she could count on one hand, and this was just the cherry on her crap cake. Of course, if she were going to be pulled over it would be by the sheriff, her blinking boss. And how's that for ironic anyway? She'd only agreed to help her friend Rebecca's mom out because she needed some space *from* the law.

Ha, the joke was on her.

Rebecca had conveniently forgotten to mention Angie worked at the county sheriff's office. By the
~~~

time Laurel realized just what she would be doing it was too late. She'd spent the last of her admittedly meager savings fixing her car up in order to make the trip from Miami. And it was all to no avail. Her uncle had still managed to follow her to town and set up his latest scam. There was no escape now. All she could do was try and minimize the damage without ending up behind bars herself.

"Are you going to answer me?" That voice. The deep, dark, mesmerizing timbre of his voice had featured in more than a few of Laurel's overnight fantasies of late. Combine that with a body built like a tank and a set of handcuffs and…

"*Miss Thomas*."

His impatience woke her up to her very real predicament. Either she came up with a plausible answer now, or she could very likely end up spending the night in an interrogation room. Not that she would mind sharing a room with the big bad sheriff, but one with a bed would be preferable. Wait, did she really just think that? Obviously, it'd been too long since she had a meaningful relationship—hashtag sex.

"Sorry, boss, it won't happen again." She almost smiled at the annoyance that flared in his chocolate brown eyes. They'd managed to strike sparks off each other ever since she started almost two months ago. She enjoyed pushing his buttons to see if she could make him lose that composed demeanor he wore like a mantle around his shoulders. The guy needed to loosen up. Life was too short to waste it all on responsibilities. Heaven knew, she'd done more than her share of time at that particular shrine.

"You need winter tires on that piece of… metal," he warned her. "And slow down. I realize where you come from snow is not an issue, but it is here. I don't have the time or the manpower to be pulling you out of some ditch every time you feel the need to push the limit."

She almost slapped her hand up in a salute at his tone of command, but thought better of it at the last second. Her daddy didn't raise no dummy.

"Okay, well, fun as this has been, I really need to get going. My boss is something of a stickler for efficiency. Maybe you've met him?" She leaned in as though she'd just imparted a state secret, breathing in the fresh clean scent of his aftershave and was that—coffee? Her mouth salivated, whether it was for the hunky male standing before her, or a shot of nirvana in the form of some much-needed caffeine she wasn't sure. Who was she kidding? Of course it was for the coffee.

Jack stared at her like she was a head-case, which she absolutely was… not.

"If you're done with the wisecracks, you can drive—slowly—to Gus's Garage and I'll see about getting that heater fixed. You can't go around all winter without a defrost cycle in that piece of crap you call a car." He squinted into the face of the growing storm and swore. "This weather's not going to lighten up any in the near future. I'll follow you in. Do you know where it is?"

Laurel's back stiffened in outrage. Who did he think he was? If she wanted her car fixed, she'd get it fixed. She didn't need some hotshot telling her what to do. She got enough of that from home.

Rather than arguing with him, Laurel climbed behind the wheel and started the engine, waiting for its high-pitched scream to wind down so she could drive. She pulled her Visa card out of her wallet and proceeded to scrape the frost off the inside of the windows. Who said credit cards aren't recyclable?

When she'd made a patch large enough to see out of, Laurel shifted into gear, and only then allowed herself a glance at the glowering hulk standing outside her door. She rolled the window down just enough to be heard.

"Sure, I know where Gus's is, but I don't need him. I can see just fine." The car rolled forward a couple of inches, as anxious to escape as she was. "Catch you back at the office, Boss."

Then she punched the gas and gasped as the car slid sideways and narrowly missed clipping Jack with the rear fender. Laurel laughed, straightened out the wheels and took off down the road in a flurry of snow.

CHAPTER TWO

By the time she pulled into the snow-laden parking lot at the sheriff's office, Laurel's temper had cooled along with the temperature outside. She shivered as she hurried toward the front doors. Her synthetic fur jacket was poor protection against the biting wind. And she'd left southern Florida for this. Maybe she *was* just as crazy as the rest of her eccentric family.

Head down to protect her uncovered face, she rounded the corner of the building and ran straight into a bulky chest. She would have bounced backward if not for the gloved hands that reached out and grasped her arms.

The startled laugh died in her throat when she looked up and met the gaze of the very man she'd been avoiding for the last week and a half, her Uncle Max.

"There you be, I've been lookin' for ya everywhere, me darlin'." His Irish heritage rang through his voice and in the ruddy handsomeness of his face. Blessed with bright blue eyes and thick dark hair, Max had never lacked charisma. Integrity, yes, charisma, no.

Her heart pounding, Laurel gave him a quick hug and stepped out of his reach, sending a nervous glance over her shoulder. She needed to get rid of him before anyone spotted them together, especially Jack. He was far too perceptive not to notice the family resemblance, even though her coloring was much fairer than that of the Black Irish side of the family. They all shared the same high cheekbones and stubborn chins. Max was her mother's older brother and took his duties as patriarch seriously. Laurel just wished he would find an honest way of supporting all of them instead of what he'd chosen for a living—scam artist extraordinaire.

"Uncle Max, what are you doing here?" She wanted to scream her frustration. Why couldn't he have worked his dirty schemes back home and left her out of it for a change?

"Well, lass, where else would I be? We're a team, you and I, we needs ta stick together." His tone was placating, but his eyes held a crafty sparkle within their depths.

Yeah, he needed her to save his butt whenever he got in over his head, which was like—always.

"Did you follow me this morning?" she asked, her head tipped to the side suspiciously.

He looked genuinely confused. "No. If'n I'd followed ya, I'd a known where you was, wouldn't I?"

Laurel sighed. The old goat had a good heart; he just couldn't resist running his get-rich quick schemes—most of which left them poorer than when they'd started. But lying to the family wasn't one of his many faults, so that meant he was telling the truth about following her. All of which left her wondering, who *had* been chasing her?

Whoever it was, they'd almost run her off the road before she managed to lose them. Her old car might not look like much, but it had a kickass motor under its hood thanks to her brother, Gabe.

"Let's go for a coffee, Uncle. I don't know about you but I'm freezing." Laurel turned and led the way back to her car, anxious to leave before the sheriff arrived.

"Don't you have to get to work?" Max huffed as he struggled to keep up with her long strides.

Yeah, she did. "It's okay, my boss is a pussycat." More like a mountain lion. One prepared to pounce on his prey at the least sign of weakness. She refused to allow that to happen to either Max or herself.

They'd just started across the parking space, escape in sight under a growing mound of fluffy white stuff, when a cruiser pulled into the lot.

Damn.

She was tempted to ignore Jack and leave anyway, but one look at his grim visage changed her mind. She couldn't afford to let him think she was hiding anything, or anyone.

"Let me handle this, Uncle Max." *Please, oh please, don't screw this up.*

"Whatever you say, darlin'," he agreed, his eyes fixed on the big man climbing out of the cop car.

Laurel set her hands on her hips and faced the sheriff with false bravado, chin in the air.

"Hey, boss." She might as well fire the opening salvo.

He hesitated, then tipped his hat back on his forehead and ignored her to check her uncle out. The two men sized each other up as though they were prizefighters about to go a few rounds in the cage. Keeping his gaze fixed on the older man, Jack unbuttoned his coat far enough to make sure Max saw his badge.

Laurel stiffened. She hurried into speech to bridge the lengthening silence. "Sheriff, this is my Uncle Max. Max, this is my *boss*." She emphasized the last word in an attempt to stop the upcoming skirmish. Not that it worked.

"Sheriff, mighty fine town you have 'ere." Max thrust out his hand. "Too bad you've bin ahavin' so much trouble with the criminal element."

"Max," Laurel warned, and shrugged when Jack gave her the look. "He didn't hear it from me."

It wasn't her fault the townspeople liked to gossip, especially with sensationalist stories including local celebrities like the Fowlers. A fatal incident and abduction at the Twilight Theatre just after Laurel arrived in town had provided plenty of chin-wagging at the Grits and Grace Cafe.

Jack let go of her uncle's hand and pointed toward her car. "I thought you might rethink getting your car seen to, so I went around by Gus's, but *no,* apparently you like freezing to death."

Max turned her way. "What's wrong, luv? I thought Gabriel gave her an overhaul before you left home?"

Laurel noticed Jack's lowering brows and hastened to change the subject. "I'm going for a coffee break to Grace's, boss. Want me to bring you back anything?"

Just as she'd hoped, her words got Jack's dander up. "What do you mean, you're going for coffee? You haven't even started work yet."

Suppressing her grin, she eased away while tugging on Max's arm. "No worries, I'll catch up in no time." Her relief at escaping without an interrogation was short-lived.

"While you're out, stop at Gus's. I told him to expect you."

Dratted man.

~~~*~~~

Jack ignored the snow drifting down around him while he watched Laurel and her uncle haphazardly clean off her car before jumping in and starting the engine. The ugly little car had something big under the hood, given away by the throaty growl when she fired it up.

There was something funny going on with those two. She'd practically tugged the old man's arm off trying to make their escape. And why hadn't she mentioned anything about having family nearby? Jack wasn't even sure where her home was. He didn't
~~~

remember Angie mentioning it when she'd come to him with the fait accompli of a new hire while she went off on a long awaited vacation.

Laurel gave the car some gas and spun the wheels. He hid his grin behind a frown and crossed his arms over his chest. She let off the throttle and glided slowly past with a little wave and toot of a sickly sounding horn. Then they were around the corner and gone, the snow quickly erasing any sign of her presence.

As if it would be that easy.

Ever since she'd shown up in his office with her crazy pile of sticky notes she liked to plaster on every available surface, he hadn't been able to get her off his mind. She irritated him with her disorganization. He was used to having a place for everything, and everything in its place, but with Laurel, that rule went out the window.

He was intrigued with her secretive honey-colored eyes, sleek womanly body, and long golden-red hair. He didn't like the churning inside whenever she was near and was determined to avoid her, but still seemed to find excuses to be close. His threatening glares warned off any would-be suitors in the department, much to his embarrassment and his staff's delight. Everyone expected him to ask her out, but Jack refused to get involved. He'd pegged Laurel for high maintenance with her fancy clothes and girly ways. He'd been down that road and had the daughter to prove it, so no thanks.

And besides, who the hell was Gabriel?

CHAPTER THREE

Laurel watched her uncle pour half a bottle of maple syrup over a stack of plate-sized pancakes topped with three sunny-side eggs, and shuddered. Any appetite she had for her own breakfast of French toast disappeared. She pushed the dish aside and reached for her coffee, cradling the cup in still cold fingers.

"Not hungry, girlie?" Max asked around a mouthful of food.

She smiled over his obvious enjoyment with the sweet feast. The way he ate he should weigh a ton, instead his waist was as trim as that of an active man half his age. It wasn't fair.

"Maybe later. So, are you going to tell me why you were looking for me earlier?" she asked.

Max finished chewing, set his fork down, and wiped his glistening lips on a napkin before meeting her gaze. “It’s your cousin, Bethany. She’s gotten herself into a wee bit of a fix. I’m afraid I’m going to need you on this one, Laurel.” His eyes were grim, unsmiling. Laurel’s heart plummeted.

“Oh, Uncle Max, what happened?” She reached across the table and grasped his gnarled, slightly sticky fingers. It was easy to forget he was almost sixty until you noticed those knotty knuckles and the faint lines bisecting his top lip. Bethany was his only daughter and the apple of her daddy’s eye. She was Laurel’s age and a good person, but seemed to attract bad luck like a bear to honey.

“That bloody husband of hers has been gambling behind her back.” Max shook his head in despair. “I tried to warn ‘er, but she was smitten. He overspent at the craps and put their house up for collateral. Now they need to come up with sixty grand or lose their home.”

Sixty grand. While that might not seem like much to some people, for Laurel it would be akin to winning the lottery—or getting hit by lightning.

"I knew that guy was a creep. So, what's she going to do?"

"Not her, my dear, us," Max answered. His blue eyes turned devilish with the gleam of a born swindler. He glanced around the half-full restaurant before leaning over the table, jeopardizing his clean, white dress shirt in the process.

"I've found my mark. I just need you to back me up. It will be like the old days. In and out, with nary a ripple." He squeezed her hand, then let it go to pick up his cup of tea. Max swore tea was the secret to longevity, and looking at him it was hard to argue the point.

Interesting what he thought was nary a ripple. Twice, they'd been run out of different little towns just when Laurel thought about calling them home. And then there was the time they had actually been arrested, and it was only through sheer good luck, and cousin Heather's judicial skills, that they escaped without a record. If he considered that smooth sailing, she hated to see what a storm would look like.

Laurel eyed her uncle over her cup and tried to come up with a diplomatic way of saying, “Hell, no.”

“Now don’t look at me that way, missy. I know what you’re thinking.”

No, you don’t.

“You’re wondering why we ever quit.”

Laurel frowned in disbelief.

Her uncle nodded his head, taking her silence for agreement. “I sometimes wonder that me-self, but it was time. You kids needed to branch out on your own, see what the world holds and I was ready to retire, maybe even go fishing for a while.”

He fiddled with his fork on the side of his plate for a moment or two, then lifted suspiciously moist eyes. “She’s my only child, Laurel, I have to help her. Please.”

She had a feeling she was getting swindled by the swindler, but what could she do? Family takes care of family; it was a Doyle clan motto she couldn’t break. If only there were a bank out there somewhere willing to give a high risk client a loan. With her lack of stability and zero assets, no one would touch her. She'd tried.

Laurel sighed and gave in to the inevitable. "So, what's the plan?"

~~~*~~~

Jack rattled around the precinct for a couple of hours, waiting out the storm. He'd written up a few reports and left them on his absent receptionist's desk for filing—whenever she deemed to show up for work. Then he'd finished preparing his case for court on the recent abduction and assault of his brother's girlfriend, Katy Fowler, and the manslaughter of old Doc Johnson. Jack was glad Ty had finally won the girl. He'd been in love with Katy since the two of them were teens. They deserved their happy ever after.

Then, he'd spent some time on the computer working two missing person's cases, with little success. Ty had asked him to run a search of adoption records for a baby boy that Katy had given up years ago. The open files had shown nothing, and he
~~~

couldn't access the sealed archives without a warrant. Maybe they'd have to look into private investigative companies to get the information. He had a few connections and would make some calls on his brother's behalf. Jack had a feeling the kid was Ty's and wanted to help however he could.

The other case was proving to be just as frustrating. It had already been two months since he'd been thrust into the middle of an international case of drug and ammunitions trafficking, when associates of the organization terrorized citizens of Tidal Falls. During the ensuing takedown, an undercover member of the DEA, Maggie Holt, was captured and never found. Jack was contacting any informant sources he could think of to assist in tracking her down. Ty's friend, Jared, had a stake in the case, as it was his old SEAL teammate's partner who had disappeared. So far they had found little to prove she was still alive, but the team refused to give up hope.

A glance out the window showed the storm was losing its grip on the area, thank God. He hadn't looked forward to spending the night patrolling the highway in search of accidents and possible fatalities. Tina still had another hour for school before he needed to picked her up and deliver her to her job at The Craft Shack. His sixteen-year-old daughter was as stubborn as her dear old dad and determined to go to university right out of high school. She'd was already saving toward that goal. Now, if only she'd give up dating.

A light tap on the office door heralded the arrival of Jack's deputy, Sid Carmichael. His scrawny shoulders under the heavy blue police jacket were piled with clumps of melting snow.

"Shee-it, that's some nasty weather out there." Sid pulled off his hat and smacked it against his thigh. "Sure am glad it's quitting soon. How'd you make out, Chief?" He dug around in pocket after pocket until he finally came up with a linen hankie. He lifted it to his nose and gave a blast loud enough to blow his brains out, and with a last couple swipes plopped down into the chair across from Jack's desk.

Jack slid the hand sanitizer toward his deputy and frowned at the water dripping onto his freshly polished tile flooring. "Yeah, it's a bad one alright. Handed out a few violation tickets and read the riot act to a speed-demon." He withheld the fact that he knew the culprit, or that it was his own receptionist.

"I swear, the worse the storm, the more idiots come out of the woodwork." Sid shook his head before glancing back through the open doorway to the quiet front end. "Mike and Norm still out then?"

"Yeah, they pulled short straw, working through the night." Jack picked up his pen and set it down again, already guessing who his friend would ask about next.

"What about Laurel? Shouldn't she be here by now?"

Bingo.

"Miss Thomas stepped out for an early break with her uncle, who I gather is in town for a short visit." Jack was pretty sure he was the only one still calling her by her surname. Her name on his lips made him feel things he wasn't ready to acknowledge. It was safer to maintain a distance between them. She threatened his placid, everyday life, and he didn't like it.

Sid twirled his hat, dislodging more droplets of water. "I met him awhile ago. Nice enough guy. He's been in town for a couple of weeks now. I seen him getting real chummy with Grace the other day." He shifted in his seat. "Hope he don't hurt her, boss. She's been alone a long time now. It would be easy to be taken advantage of." He looked up, and then quickly away again.

Holy shit, he's in love with Grace Martin.

Jack sank back in his seat flabbergasted. He definitely hadn't seen the writing on that wall. But he agreed with Sid anyway. Grace was a much-beloved part of the community—mess with her, you mess with the town. He better do a little digging around on Uncle Max.

CHAPTER FOUR

By the time Laurel listened to her uncle's harebrained scheme, tried to talk him out of it—with no luck—and drove him to The Rendezvous Hotel where he'd been staying, she was seriously late getting back to work. The only good news in her craptastic day so far, was that the storm had finally loosened its grip on the turbulent skies.

She couldn't believe the mess she was in. Her family needed her help and she felt obligated since they'd always been there for her and her mother. But on the other hand, Laurel really liked this town—and its surly sheriff. She didn't want to run any more.

When she'd tried to explain this to Max, all he said was, "We'll be careful, luv. They'll never know you had a part in it at all."

Sure.

That had worked well in the past—not. And Grace was so sweet and kind. How could Uncle Max even consider swindling her? He'd actually been proud of the fact he already had her nibbling his carefully baited hook of a lonely old man down on his luck. Another week or two, he said, and he would have her caught on his line and ready to land in the net. Which is where she was expected to drop the '*oh so shocking*' news of her uncle's imminent need of a costly surgery they couldn't afford to pay for. A few crocodile tears later and they'd hopefully be on the road to Florida with a large cash donation in their possession. *If* everything went according to plan.

Laurel yanked on the heavy glass door and entered the foyer of the sheriff's office. She stomped her feet on the rubber mat to dislodge snow, and maybe some of her temper. It wouldn't accomplish anything to get mad, she knew that. But sometimes…

"So you decided to grace us with your presence after all."

She jumped and let out a little screech, her hands flapping in the air like a beheaded chicken's wings. The damn man did it on purpose, she knew he did.

"I was just thinking about getting together a search party." Jack's imposing figure filled the doorway. It took a minute or two for Laurel's heart to slowly settle. She glared in his direction as she hung up her jacket and wrapped her scarf around the hook, wishing it were someone's neck instead.

"Did you have to startle me like that? I told you I'd make it up to you." She tried to move past, but he wasn't going anywhere, so she was forced to take a step back out of his space. He leaned one massive shoulder against the doorframe and crossed his ankle over one booted foot, obviously in no hurry to let her get to work.

Laurel couldn't help but admire his physique. Long, muscular legs were encased in well-worn jeans that fit him like a glove. A rugged face with eyes that saw too much topped a blue uniform dress shirt rolled up revealed forearms covered in a smattering of dark hair.

"What?" His silence put her on the defensive, making her nervous. She dug around in her handbag until she located her gum.

"Want a piece?" He quirked a brow at her offer and she shrugged, embarrassed at her word choice.

"So, your uncle, huh?" His espresso-colored eyes followed her every move. Laurel stilled, the stick of spearmint halfway to her mouth. Then with forced nonchalance she smiled and slipped the gum between suddenly dry lips. Jack's gaze narrowed.

"Look, I'm sorry I took off like that, but my uncle hasn't been well lately and I… I worry about him." She glanced up to see if he was buying any of this, but his face was noncommittal, so she hurried on, "He raised me and my brother after my dad died. I was still pretty young then." At least that part was true. "Mom tried, but it was too hard to find childcare she could afford for two children on a minimum wage job. She had to ask her brother for help. Uncle Max insisted we move in with him and his daughter, Bethany. My Aunt Joan had passed away years earlier so it was just the two of them."

Laurel blinked rapidly and coughed to clear the lump in her throat. Much as the Doyle family lived under a different code of ethics from her own, she still loved them with all her heart.

Jack straightened from the wall and took a step forward. His hand came up and brushed her mussed hair back from her face, his palm a rough caress against her suddenly heated cheek. He tipped her chin up until he could see into her eyes.

"Don't apologize. Family is more important than answering some phones for me," he teased, reminding her of when she first started and couldn't keep up to the phone calls coming into the office. "I think it's commendable that you are so close to your uncle. If you need a few days off while he's in town, let me know, I'm sure we can make some sort of arrangement."

There he was being the nice guy again. Why couldn't he be a jerk so that she wouldn't feel so bad about lying to him? Stupid tears floated to the surface though she tried to squelch them.

Jack frowned and used his thumb to sweep them away. "Hey now, none of that. I'm not firing you, if that's what you're thinking."

Laurel tried to laugh, but it came out more like a burble. Why did this have to happen now? She'd finally found a job she enjoyed in a town she wanted to call home along with a growing attraction to the man standing in front of her with the body of a Greek god and the heart of a pussycat. And in another couple of weeks it was all going to come crashing down around her ears.

"Thanks, boss." The urge to wrap her arms around him and burrow into his broad chest was oh-so-tempting, but that would only make an already complicated situation that much worse. She bravely lifted her eyes to meet his gaze—and gulped. He was fixated on her lips. Her tongue reflexively flicked out to lick their dryness and his pupils dilated. Laurel's breath suspended in her throat.

"This isn't a good idea," she whispered as his head lowered.

"Probably not," he agreed just before he consumed her, there was no other word for it. She'd been kissed before, but never like this. There was nothing but Jack. From the faint spicy scent of his cologne paired with the impossible width of his shoulders, to the exquisite firmness of his mouth upon hers.

Laurel grabbed his forearms and held on for dear life, caught up in a maelstrom of desire she was powerless to resist. He tasted like the finest chocolate, wickedly delicious and oh-so-bad for her health. This couldn't end well for either of them, but she couldn't bring herself to step back.

Soon. Soon, she would have to, she knew that.

Just a little more.

~~~*~~~

Jack was losing his mind. He had to be. What other excuse could there be for him to accost his employee in a public foyer? Crazy. She'd cast a spell over him, one he was loath to break. What other reason could there be for this insane urge to hold her in his arms and protect her from the world?
~~~

Her lips were soft, like her creamy skin. They tasted like sweet, tart cherries, and reminded him of her personality. She seemed so small and delicate within his embrace, but the grip she had on his arms and the fire sparking in her eyes showed him her inner core of strength. It ignited a conflagration in his body he had to fight to resist. He craved to feel her passion burning him alive.

The last time he'd felt an all-consuming desire such as this, it had proven to be his destruction. The reminder of his ex-wife was enough to bring him to his senses. This was a mistake. Jack didn't lose control any longer. He'd learned his lesson the hard way. He eased away, his lips clinging, reluctant to part company with such temptation.

Her sandy colored eyelashes fluttered before languidly opening to reveal golden brown eyes hazy with lust. She blinked a couple of times, then straightened, her hands falling away from his body. Jack felt the loss keenly.

Shit.

He didn't need this right now. His life was crazy enough with a teenage daughter to raise, not to mention the demanding duties of his position as sheriff of a town facing growing pains. He valued normalcy and regularity in his everyday life. There was nothing wrong with a peaceful—okay, dull—existence; he liked his world to operate that way.

"What did you do that for?" Anger had replaced the soft look of desire in her face, turning her cheeks rosy, which in turn highlighted the smattering of freckles across the bridge of her cute button nose.

Jack would have smiled except he wondered the same thing himself.

"Consider it a momentary aberration. It won't happen again."

I hope.

"It better not," Laurel snapped, her coppery red mane glowing with static electricity—or temper, he wasn't sure which. "Now if you'll excuse me, I have work to do." She brushed by him and fiery tendrils of her hair whipped out as though attempting to flay him.

"Some of us can't stand around doing nothing all day, you know." Her parting words as she flounced into the office worked like nothing else could have.

Jack burst out laughing like he hadn't done in a very long time.

CHAPTER FIVE

Laurel hummed along with the tunes playing over the radio while she decorated the office's Charlie Brown Christmas tree. She'd turned the worst side against the wall, but it was still adorably ugly. It kind of reminded her of one of the older deputies, Sid Carmichael. Skinny and knobby-kneed, it bowed at an awkward angle and looked ready to crash to the floor at any moment, so she tied it with silver garland and hooked it to the coatrack. There, much better. She stood back and grinned.

The outside door clanged open and a teenage girl burst through laughing at something behind her. Make that someone. Jack followed her in, brushing what was left of a well-aimed snowball off his chest.

"Lucky shot," he said, and tossed a chunk of ice in her direction.

"No fair, Daddy. You said first one in wins," Tina gasped. She whirled away, only to come to a sliding halt when she noticed the tree. "Hey, that's supposed to be my job. I do the Christmas tree every year." She glared at Laurel.

"Tina, you know better than to be rude. Apologize." Jack's brows rose in surprise.

Laurel turned away, embarrassed to have caused a scene. "It's okay, Sheriff. I wouldn't have started this if I'd known." She moved to the radio and shut it off, and was immediately sorry she had, because the silence was so much more awkward than listening to "Rudolf, the Red-nosed Reindeer."

She chanced a glance at Jack's stern countenance, decided absence was the better part of valor and hurried toward the filing room, but stopped before she'd taken more than a couple of strides. She'd dreamed of having moments like she'd just witnessed between the Garrett's with her own father. She wasn't sure what to say to end the animosity between them, but she had to try.

Nostalgic memories rushed to the front of her mind. “The last time I decorated a Christmas tree I was six.”

Her brother, Gabriel, had loved to throw handfuls of tinsel at the branches. Her mother always laughed and rearranged the clumps into colorful dripping icicles. Her father had the important job of climbing the ladder to place the angel on the very top while the woodsy scent of the fresh cut pine filled the room. But best of all, Laurel recalled her parents dancing in front of the newly lit sparkling tree, eyes filled with the light of love. That was the last time she remembered truly being happy. Her father had died not long after that Christmas.

She turned and faced the sullen teen. “I’m truly sorry for ruining a special tradition you share with your father. Just take off the decorations I added and start fresh, I haven’t done too much yet anyway.”

“Tina didn’t mean to be so rude. Right, Tina?” Jack prodded his girl.

Her brown eyes, so like her dad's, glistened. "No," she mumbled. "I'm sorry." She dropped her head and scuffed the toes of her UGGS so they squeaked on the linoleum.

Laurel avoided the compassionate look in Jack's eyes. The last thing she wanted to do was come between father and daughter.

"Okay, well then, I'll just be in the filing room if you need me, boss." She added the moniker as much for him as for his daughter. Things had been a bit tense between them the past few days since their… encounter. She couldn't even think about it without becoming hot and flustered. The man knew how to kiss that's for sure, which led to the interesting question of what else was he good at?

Not that she planned on finding out, of course. She could already see the headlines—'*Felon in bed with Lawman*,' news at six.

With a last reassuring smile at the teen, Laurel turned away intent on giving father and daughter their quality time together, but Tina's voice stopped her forward momentum.

"You can stay if you want."

Laurel hesitated, torn between the longing to be included in their world, if only for a little while, and escape.

"C'mon, Laur… Miss Thomas, we could use your help. I seriously suck at untangling strings of lights." The laughing appeal in Jack's words sealed the deal. After all, what could be more innocent than decorating a tree in a police station with a teenager and her way too appealing father?

~~~*~~~

Jack told himself he was just being a good cop. There was something going on with his receptionist and her elderly uncle, but so far he hadn't managed to question her about Max, possibly because he'd done everything in his power to avoid her since their encounter last week.

Laurel had shaken him with her response to his kiss. His loss of control embarrassed him. He never crossed the line with the people he worked with; at least he hadn't until now. But, he'd known from the
~~~

moment he laid eyes on her that first day she was going to be trouble.

His men had surrounded her like bees to honey. Then he got his first glimpse and realized why. She was like Marilyn Monroe in Technicolor. Tendrils of copper colored hair pulled up in a no nonsense bun slipped down around the alabaster skin of her neck and flirted with the collar of her snowy white blouse. Pearly teeth worried lush, full lips outlined in coral pink lip-gloss.

The closer Jack strode to the counter the more he'd wondered what Angie, his regular receptionist, had been smoking when she hired the debutante to fill the position while she was away. Post-it notes adorned every surface in cheerful abandon, reminders covering all aspects of the job. Reminders she wouldn't need if she were as experienced as he'd been led to believe.

But the instant he'd met her intelligent golden brown eyes and saw more than the flirty, slightly disorganized secretary, Jack's interest was well and truly caught. What brought a woman who looked like a pin-up girl all the way from Florida to Washington? So far as he knew, all of her family resided in the Sunshine State. Admittedly, there were days when he'd like to be a few thousand miles away from his brother and two sisters, not to mention his parents, various aunts, uncles and cousins, all of who resided in Tidal Falls. But, this was home. He loved it here and couldn't imagine a better place to raise his daughter.

Laurel's laughter drew him out of his musings. Jack shook his head at the silly, sexy image of her with an elf's hat perched precariously upon her head, curls peeping from beneath the brim. She was smiling at something Tina had just said, a box of shiny Christmas balls in her hand. He swallowed a lump of tenderness at the care she was taking to draw his daughter out of her funk. It hadn't been easy not having a mom for Tina. He'd done the best he could, and his sisters, Ashley and Bear—Bernadette—were great with her, but nothing could take the place of a real mother.

He'd thought himself in love almost from the moment he slept with April Montgomery. Smart, beautiful, crazy. Too bad he didn't pick up on that last one until it was too late. She was pregnant and begging for marriage, and he'd given in for all the wrong reasons. Not long before Tina was born he'd been offered a football scholarship at Penn State, a dream come true. April was thrilled, her stature in the community guaranteed. But the more he made, the more she spent. And then she started staying out at night, socializing, she called it. He had another name for it. Their fights over the issue had culminated in a car accident that ended him and his buddy, Mitch Taylor's careers. And then she left.

"Are you just going to watch us, Daddy, or are you going to help?" Tina stood grinning quizzically at him, her hands on her narrow jean clad hips.

Jack's mouth quirked. No one did attitude like his girl. "I was waiting on you two hens to quit clucking so we could get down to work," he teased.

"Sure, you were. Did you know daydreaming is an early sign of the onset of dementia?" She threw him a string of lights and he grimaced at the knotted mess.

"I thought I taught you to respect your elders?" he said, and grinned at Laurel's sputtered laughter. "See, Miss Thomas agrees."

She shook her head and the hat slid south. A quick catch righted its position. She handed the glass ornaments over to Tina and picked up a second one from the supplies. "Leave me out of this, you two. I'm just an impartial observer."

She turned and carefully hung a shiny red bell on one of the nearby branches, giving it a little flick with her fingertip that resounded through his core. A snow globe of a festive village followed, then she lifted a blue velvet Santa from the box and stood for a moment contemplating the best location. Jack was about to suggest a bare spot on a lower branch when she stretched up on a death defying pair of candy apple red heels and damn near stopped his breath. Her modest, knee-length skirt slid inch-by-tantalizing-inch up her thighs, revealing shapely legs and a taut heart-shaped derriere. Her furry white sweater lifted to play peek-a-boo with a cherry blossom branch tattooed onto the small of her back. Jack's fingers itched to touch the engraved symbol of feminine strength. His mouth watered with the urge to nuzzle her neck below her raised chin. To turn her into his arms and pick up where they'd left off. To...

"Dad, you're making it worse."

Tina's voice jarred him awake. What was he doing fantasizing with his daughter right there in the room? And over someone who probably wouldn't even stick around until spring either. He glanced down and saw the jangled mess he'd made of the lights and swore under his breath.

CHAPTER SIX

Laurel nestled the tattered old Santa into place on the branch, careful to avoid the sharp needles and sank down from her toes for a better look. Perfect. She overheard Tina giving her dad a hard time over the lights and had to smile. It reminded her of happier times spent with her own family. It was obvious Tina and her father had a close connection to each other. Rumor was Jack's wife had left him and Tina the moment his career as a pro football star ended due to a terrible auto accident.

She couldn't imagine ever walking away from her own child like that, never mind leaving a great guy like Jack Garrett. Not only was he clearly devoted to his daughter, he worked hard to take care of his town. And the man was seriously hot. His nutmeg brown hair had a slight curl that invited a woman's hands while his chiselled face and expressive eyes said he'd know how to make her happy. Laurel felt her nipples harden and glanced over her shoulder to make sure no one was paying any attention to her.

Jack's gaze was focused on her butt. She flushed and hurried to swipe her fingers down the back of her skirt in case some tinsel clung there or something. Nope, not a thing, but her movement did achieve results. Now Jack's attention lifted to her face with an intensity that had her hands going damp.

Wow.

The man had sinful intentions written all over him in broad strokes. If only she dared to take him up on it, but that would be the height of stupidity. He stood for upholding justice, while she… she hoisted the flag for allegiance. It wouldn't work. Besides, she was leaving soon anyway, thanks to Max.

"How's your uncle making out?" Jack asked.

Laurel jumped. *Does he know?*

She pulled herself together. Of course not, he was just being polite, making conversation. She eased out a strained breath and attempted a relaxed smile. “He’s good… most days.” It couldn’t hurt to lay the groundwork for her upcoming reveal of her uncle’s supposed dire circumstances. Laurel watched Tina place ornaments for a few moments. The guilt over what they planned sat on her chest like the flu. She hated lying to these people who’d given her a chance at a new life.

“Is he ill then?” Jack probed.

Laurel was searching for a diplomatic way to change the subject when Tina solved the problem.

“Daddy look, remember this?” She held up a circle of yellowed clay, a child’s handprint immortalized within. Jack’s face softened with parental love. He moved to his daughter’s side and wrapped an arm around her skinny shoulders, drawing her close.

“Of course, I do. That was the first Christmas gift you were old enough to make for me. Aunt Tess helped you with the mould, but you insisted on wrapping it yourself.” He smiled into her beaming face. “I'm pretty sure you used a whole roll of scotch tape on the paper, but nothing could stop me from seeing what you made. I'll treasure it always."

Laurel was surprised that they would use such a special keepsake here, in the sheriff's office. "Don't you worry about it getting broken?"

Tina was the first to reply, "I wanted Dad to have something at work to remind him to come home at night." She shrugged, looking uncomfortable with the admission.

Not so Jack. He pulled his daughter into a tight hug, before leaning back to look her in the eye. "I will *always* be around to make your life miserable, don't ever doubt that." He chucked her lightly under the chin. "It's you and me, kid, forever. Okay?"

Laurel's chest tightened. She blinked back tears. Jack was one in a million. She'd give anything to have someone's unconditional love the way the Garretts displayed theirs. Tina was a lucky girl. It would be wonderful to have a man like Jack in her corner, no matter what.

The opening beats of the latest Taylor Swift song interrupted the moment. Tina swiped her eyes, dug into her back pocket, and pulled out her cellphone. A quick glance at the screen and she turned bright red, spinning away with a muttered, “Be right back.”

Jack looked pained as he watched her twirl and un-twirl the ends of her hair while giggling at whoever was on the other end of the line. Laurel took pity on him, redirecting his attention to the tree. “Miles of forest all around us and this is the nicest pine you could find?”

Jack’s lips quirked as though she’d said something funny. He threw the jumbled pile of lights into the box and stepped around the table. When he arrived at her side he reached out and fingered the needles of the nearest branch, releasing a pungent aroma into the air between them.

“This is a spruce tree,” he said as he gazed into her eyes, humor lighting their depths. “Short needles, see? A pine’s needles are longer and softer, Florida girl.”

Laurel bristled, and then relaxed, laughing softly. “Fair enough, Ranger Rick. Next time you’re in my part of the world I’ll show you some real trees.”

His look turned liquid, melting her resistance. "I'll hold you to it."

She could totally picture him wandering the beach in board shorts—and nothing else. "I don't think you could handle the heat." The flirting was unintentional, but worked to fan the flames nonetheless.

Jack's hand moved to her waist and tugged her closer. Close enough she could feel the inferno raging beneath his skin and the rigid length of his erection. She swallowed hard.

Just as Tina was ending her call, he leaned in and whispered in her ear. "Try me."

Then he was gone, back to working those blasted lights as though his soul depended upon it.

CHAPTER SEVEN

A couple of days later Laurel wandered along Main Street enjoying the crisp air and the impossibly blue skies. A fresh layer of snow blanketed the mountain peaks in the distance, but none had fallen in town since the big storm, thank God. There wasn't much that she wasn't willing to try, but driving on icy roads was a skill she could do without. In that regard she was definitely a Florida bunny, as Jack liked to remind her every chance he had.

Since things were momentarily quiet at the office, he'd given her the afternoon off to do "girly stuff" as he'd put it. So she'd taken advantage of the opportunity to get her hair trimmed at the Hair Affair Salon, where the owner, Jenny, was more than happy to fill her ears with the local gossip. Over and above "who was cheating on who", and the latest on the most eligible bachelors in town—which of course included the sheriff—she also imparted some distressing news. Grace Martin had diabetes.

"It's the saddest thing," Jenny lamented as she tipped Laurel's head to the side so she could clip around the ears. "I've known the Martins since I was an itty bitty little thing. It about broke Grace's heart when Jared left town to join the Navy. I figured this would be their second chance. You know, since he's come home now and all."

No, Laurel hadn't known. She hadn't met Jared yet, but already felt a kinship with the man. She'd been looking for a do-over herself when she got the call from her old college roomie, Rebecca Sorenson. When Rebecca mentioned her mom's dream of a vacation to Nevada if only she could find a temporary replacement for her receptionist job in Washington State, half way across the country, it had seemed like fate.

Fate, ha.

The situation was quickly becoming untenable. She was being forced to choose between family loyalty and her heart. These people cared about each other, and although they knew nothing about her they'd welcomed her in without reservation. Laurel was making a home for herself here and resented the need to give it all up.

"What's the matter, honey? You know what they say about hairdressers, right?" Jenny eyed her in the mirror while gently running the comb through Laurel's still damp hair.

Laurel glanced at the cutting shears and then away, her eyes lighting on the plaque propped up on the edge of the table, *Words of Wisdom: Don't piss off your hairstylist…ever.*

Her hands turned sweaty beneath the cape. She cleared her throat before slowly answering. "The body is in the cut?"

Jenny's blue eyes, caked in matching blue eyeshadow, widened for a stunned second, before crinkling at the edges as their owner let loose a peel of laughter.

"Oh, that's good," she snickered. "The body is in the cut, I like it." She swiped at her runaway mascara, giving herself a set of raccoon eyes in the process before tapping the scissors on Laurel's shoulder.

"I was going to say, what is shared in the salon, stays in the salon. So if you ever need to talk, sugar-pie, I'm here, okay?" The women's eyes met in a moment of solidarity, then Jenny went back to work, tipping Laurel's head this way and that and snipping here and there.

Laurel sat in the chair and fought the overwhelming urge to spill her guts. So much of her focus in life had been spent trying to pay back her uncle for his kindness that she'd never taken the time to make any deep connections with anyone else. Even Rebecca didn't know the whole story. No one did.

~~~*~~~

Jack met up with his deputies, Mike Randolph and Norm Walters, in the parking lot of The Rendezvous Hotel.

"This the car you were telling me about?" he asked, as the three of them stood watching Gus back
~~~

the tow-truck into position behind a dirty green four-door Chevy Impala.

"Yeah, that's it," Mike nodded, his cheeks ruddy from the cold. "We waited right here like you asked. No sign of the owner."

"Has someone checked with Pearl already to see if it's registered to one of her guests?" Jack questioned, his attention on the out of state plates. Florida. Now if he were a man who believed in coincidences, this wouldn't matter as much. But since he was a cynical bastard, he kind of had to wonder at the chances of three different citizens of the land of sunshine and lollipops showing up here in his little town—in the middle of freaking winter. Something wasn't adding up, and he *hated* puzzles.

Norm looked at him like he had a screw loose, which was highly possible. After all, he'd hired her. *Her* of course being the current stealer of his dreams, his own fantasy girl, Laurel Thomas.

"I'm not the one with my head in the clouds. There's something fishy going on and all you can think about is getting into our secretary's pants. Mind you, if I got my hands on that ass I'd…" Norm's words were cut off when Jack let out a roar and charged, driving him back against the side of his squad car with a shoulder to the gut.

"Shut the fuck up, you don't know what you're talking about," Jack ground out between clenched teeth.

"I know you got it bad if you can't see there's something weird going on around here." Norm shoved Jack's larger frame off and glared at him.

Mike stepped in the middle, taking his life in his hands since both men outweighed him by at least fifty pounds or more. "C'mon, you guys are friends. Cool down and talk it out. We aren't going to figure nothing out if you keep going around half-cocked."

Jack eyed Norm over Mike's head. There'd been friendly rivalry between the two men before over women, but nothing like this. The thought of Norm anywhere near Laurel made him see red. He wanted to snort like a bull. Shit, his heart was pounding. And all over a woman who wouldn't even be around in time for spring. He was an idiot.

Jack stepped back, lifting his hands to show he was done. He heaved out a heavy breath, clouding the air in front of him, then turned back to inspecting the Impala, determined to let the matter drop.

"Pearl says the car's been sitting here a week. That dates back to the blizzard we got last Monday," Norm said quietly.

Relieved that his friend intended to follow his cue, Jack moved closer and peered into the frosty glass. A collection of fast food containers and several gas station coffee cups sat discarded on the passenger seat and floor space. He could just make out a pile of receipts crumpled in the console.

There was a clang as the winch cable was released on the tow truck. Jack strode to the rear of the car and waited while Gus hooked onto the sub-frame and loaded the car onto the flatbed. When he was done Gus hopped down from the cab and hurried toward them, his salt and pepper hair giving him a dour look.

"Thanks, Jack. Where do you think the owner is?"

Yeah, that was the million-dollar question. The car was far from fancy, but still… Unless it was stolen, he'd have to assume foul play. The containers seemed to suggest the car was in use when the subject disappeared. He needed this right now like he needed a hole in the head. All roads seemed to be leading back to his receptionist and Jack didn't like it, not one bit.

CHAPTER EIGHT

By the time Laurel made it back to the little house she'd rented from Jack's aunt—though she hadn't known of the relationship at the time—the stress of the afternoon had caught up with her. It was hard to go along as though nothing was wrong. Especially when the blocks she'd spent so much time building, such as her job, friendships, and a burgeoning relationship with the sheriff and his daughter, were about to come tumbling down.

She'd just set her purse on the end table by the door when she heard a faint buzz from inside. Worried that it might be her mother, she hurried to paw through to the bottom of the handbag where everything always seemed to land. Sure enough, her cell sat buried under a pile of unpaid bills, napkins, and ew—was that the sandwich she forgot to eat at work yesterday?

She thumbed through to her most recent text messages and saw three from her mom, two from Uncle Max, and one from her cousin, Bethany. What the heck was going on now?

She kicked off her boots on the way to the sofa and sank down with a relieved sigh before opening her mom's notes.

Hi dear,

Laurel's lips twitched. It had taken sixty-five years for her mother to get a cell phone and she insisted on proper punctuation while texting.

Have you heard from your Uncle Max recently?

Not since their lunch last week.

No, Mom. What's up?

While waiting for her reply, Laurel scrolled over to her uncle's messages.

Hey, m'darlin', I need to see U

What did he do now?

What's wrong?

Lastly she moved to her cousin's message. She blanched at the stark words.

Joe knows where Daddy is. He's on his way

Crap, could her life get any more screwed up? Laurel had let Jack go with the assumption she'd been driving carelessly, when in fact someone had tried to run her off the road and she only narrowly managed to escape. And a couple of times since then her back had crawled with the feeling someone was watching her, although a careful search never revealed a thing, so she'd sluffed it off to imagination. Now she had to wonder though.

Are you okay?

She worried Bethany might have gotten in the way of her ex's fist in order for him to get that information. It wouldn't be the first time Joe hit her. A trill let Laurel know another message had just come in.

Bethany is in the hospital. That bugger messed her up pretty darn bad.

Her heart skipped a beat. Her mom never swore, not even mild profanity. That, more than anything, told her how bad it must be. Another note from Bethany arrived.

I'm in the hospital, cousin. He got so mad when I told him there was no more money. He doesn't believe me

Then, before Laurel could reply, she added,

I'm scared

Oh, Bethany. Laurel had tried to warn her about Joe a couple of times, but her cousin only saw the good in people so she'd brushed off the comments. Even when Joe started pushing her around and flirting with other women, Bethany had found ways to excuse his behaviour. It angered and frustrated her. Bethany deserved so much more than that piece of crap she'd tied herself to.

There was only one answer Laurel could give. Her fingers slid over the keypad.

I'll take care of it

~~~*~~~

An hour later an expected knock came at Laurel's front door. She double-checked through the side window first, then opened the door to her uncle,
~~~

shivering at the blast of cold air. A quick glance showed the sky darkening to a pewter grey with heavy snow-filled clouds forming on the horizon. *Didn't the crappy weather ever take a break?*

"Evening, my girl. Brr, it's colder than a witch's tit out there." His nose and cheeks were ruddy and Laurel could feel the chill in his body as she helped him off with his wool jacket.

"You need to get a parka if you plan on being here for long, Uncle." She hung up the heavy coat and ushered him into her cozy den. A few logs crackling merrily in the fireplace provided a cheerful glow and some much-needed warmth.

"Sit by the fire," she urged. "I'll bring you some tea." Max had never possessed a driver's license. He preferred to walk anywhere he needed to go, which was fine in Florida—here, not so much, unless you didn't mind going around looking like *Frosty the Snowman.*

Returning with a tray laden with camembert, crackers, her uncle's favorite oatmeal cookies and the promised pot of tea, Laurel found Max rubbing tiredly at the spot between his eyes. Her heart softened with love for the man who'd taken on the role of a father figure for her and her brother without complaint. She hated to think what might have happened otherwise. Especially with her mom contracting pneumonia not long after her father died. Child Services were looking into placing them in foster care when her uncle stepped in and invited them into his home.

"I'm guessing by the look on your face that you heard the news," she said quietly, setting the tray down on the footstool between them before sinking cross-legged to the floor.

"If you be talking about my sweet Bethany, yes child, I heard." He glanced at her with a sadness that made her ache inside, then turned back to his contemplation of the flames. "A father should be able to protect his child. I'm nothing but a failure."

Laurel had never seen her uncle look so defeated. It worried her. They needed to take care of Joe. Once and for all.

She reached over the top of the stool and gave his bony knee a pat. “Please don’t ever think that, Uncle Max. You’ve always been the yarn that holds us all together. We’d unravel without you.” She met his teary eyes and felt her own well up with emotion. “None of that now, we Doyles don’t give up, it’s not in our…”

“DNA,” he murmured at the same time as her, then faintly smiled. “I wonder where you heard that before, eh?”

Relieved that she’d managed to pull him out of his funk, if only for the moment, Laurel filled his cup with jasmine tea and passed it over. He inhaled the fragrance and sighed his pleasure.

“You make tea like your Maimeò, full-bodied and robust. Perfect for what ails ye.” He winked.

She smiled, remembering Grandma Doyle and her hooch hidden in the kitchen cupboard behind the pots and pans. Whenever she made a pot of tea she’d add a splash of rum. “For the joints,” she always said.

Laurel offered her uncle a cookie, and frowned when she accidently dropped a butter knife on the floor. "How bad is Bethany?" she asked.

Max prevaricated, pointing at the utensil. "You're going to have a man visit ye soon." He pulled a blue and white checked hankie from his pocket and swiped at his eyes before replying. "She has a broken arm, a cracked jaw, and he burst her eardrum."

Laurel sat in stunned silence. Joe's charismatic smile and laughing green eyes flashed through her mind. She'd hadn't trusted him; something about the guy never rang true with her, but this… what kind of man attacks a woman half his size? She shivered and rolled to her feet so she could add another log to the fire—and regain her composure.

"What do we do now? He's coming after us, Uncle. We need help." She turned and held out her hands, pleading to his good sense. "Let me tell the sheriff, he'll know what to do."

"No," he roared, half lifting from the armchair. His tea sloshed over the edge of his cup and settled his temper. He grunted his apology and bent over to wipe up the mess with his handkerchief, groaning over the awkward position. His face was flushed when he rose, either from exertion or anger, she wasn't sure. Where the fire's dancing shadows had seemed warm and cosy, now the crackle and pop of the burning wood just reflected the tension between Laurel and her uncle.

Max sighed and searched for a clean corner of his kerchief to wipe his forehead before slumping into his chair. "I'm too old to see the inside of a prison, don't ye see?" He gazed up at her through rheumy eyes. "We do this job, you and I, get Joe his money, and I promise on your sainted aunt's soul that I'll hang up my conman's hat for good. Deal?"

Something wasn't adding up here. Max told her before the money was for Bethany's house after Joe gambled it away, so why was he chasing across the country after them?

"What aren't you telling me? Why did Joe beat the crap out of Bethany in order to find you?" she demanded.

Max stared into the fire for a long moment, and when he turned back all the flames of hell seemed to dance in his eyes.

"He found out that I arranged for him to lose that night. I wanted him out of Bethany's life and figured if he thought she had nothing left, he'd go." Tears rolled unheeded down his cheeks and broke Laurel's heart. "I'm the reason she's in that hospital bed."

CHAPTER NINE

Jack hesitated with his hand fisted to knock on Laurel's pumpkin-colored door. His aunt had this thing about brightly painted doors being good luck, or some such hogwash. The murmur of a voice from within told him Laurel had company. *Male* company. He tapped the file in his other hand against his thigh and glared a hole through the door.

"Guess it can wait 'til morning," he grumbled, turning to step gingerly down the snow-covered stairs. Whoever-the-asshat-was, he could have at least shoveled them off for her. Just as he reached the sidewalk an angry shout coming from inside the house startled him. Jack grabbed for his service revolver and jumped for the door. He missed the stairs entirely and dropped the file, allowing it to fall unheeded into the snowbank. The papers from within tobogganed down the slope.

He rammed a fist against the wood. “Sheriff’s department, open the door.” His heart thundered in his chest and there was a ringing in his ears. Was he having a frigging heart attack for crying out loud? He’d never reacted like this before, not even when he’d chased after a murderer a few months ago. But the thought of someone hurting…

“Laur…el,” he shouted, panic clawing the back of his throat. Jack tried the knob but it was locked. He took a step back, angled himself sideways, and prepared to slam his shoulder into the wood. He started forward, slipping a little on the icy deck boards. Good thing, because it slowed him down just enough to narrowly avoid ploughing Laurel over when she pulled the door open.

“Hello?”

When she saw him barrelling toward her with a gun in hand her beautiful eyes took over her face. “Yee…ahh,” she cried, tumbling backward and smacking her head against the now swinging door.

Fuuuck.

Jack tried backpedalling, but the slippery footing beneath his cowboy boots—dumb choice of footwear—had him sailing right into her already off-balanced body.

"Laurel, holy shit." His hand reached out to grip her shoulder, conscious of the soft womanly feel of her plastered against his rapidly hardening body. Great. "I'm sorry, honey. Are you okay?"

~~~*~~~

Stunned, Laurel nodded, flinching at the pain radiating from the back of her head. It took a moment for her eyes to uncross and realize that the weight crushing her into the door was none other than her boss. And was he happy to see her or…?

Oh yeah, a gun. She had to lift a hand to her mouth to block the nervous giggle threatening to erupt.

Jack's brow rose at her reaction. A slow smile lit his gorgeous brown eyes. "What's so funny?" he murmured, his voice a velvet rumble that reverberated in her blood, heating her from the inside out.
~~~

His head had a fine dusting of melting snowflakes, turning his hair a dark chestnut. Without thinking Laurel lifted a hand to brush her fingers through the damp curls. The air around them fairly steamed with sensual tension. Jack groaned, his gaze going dark with carnal intent.

Laurel's breath stilled, everything within her poised for the moment those oh-so-sinfully delicious lips found hers. Lights sparked behind her eyes the moment his wickedly mobile mouth took control. Her heart jumpstarted, pumping much needed oxygenated blood to her brain. What was she doing? Her uncle would be checking on her any minute now.

But then his hands found the tips of her breasts and she was lost. Her head fell backward with another thunk—this time going unnoticed—and her eyes practically rolled back in her head. Her nipples were one of her main erogenous zones, almost painfully sensitive. Most men thought they were giving pleasure when in reality it was torture. Not Jack. He played her body like it was a fine instrument, and he, a master musician. Dexterous fingers gently strummed her nerve-endings to blazing life. It was too much. It wasn't nearly enough.

"Jack." She inhaled, panting like she'd just run the Boston marathon. "Jack, we have to stop."

"Hmm?" he hummed and the vibration tickled her core and made her ache with needs and desires fated to be unfulfilled.

"My uncle is in the other room."

That got a reaction, but not the one she expected.

Instead of leaping away like a scalded cat, Jack laid his forehead alongside hers and took a few cleansing breaths before leaning back.

"You don't know how relieved I am to hear that." And then he saw her puzzled frown. "I heard a male voice when I arrived and assumed you had a man here."

As if that should explain everything.

Laurel scowled. "I do have a man here. I just told you that."

Now he was getting irritated also. He stood straight and glared into her upturned face. "Don't be an idiot," he said.

She gasped in outrage.

"I was talking about a lover, of course," he growled.

What the h-e-double-l did that mean, *of course*?

Men.

You can't live with them, and you can't shoot 'em. It's a felony.

CHAPTER TEN

Jack glared down at Laurel's tensed body and fisted hands. The ugly orange door clashed with her flushed cheeks and hair the color of autumn leaves. What just happened? One minute they were locking lips like a couple of randy teenagers and the next… hell, he wasn't sure what set her off like that. All he'd said was that he was glad it was her uncle who was visiting. No need to get all huffy.

Women.

He gave the long-suffering sigh of put upon men everywhere, and took a step back from the scowling wildcat in front of him. "I dropped a file outside when I thought you might need saving."

I should have known better.

Who would be crazy enough to mess with that temper? "I'll be right back. Maybe by then you'll have cooled down some."

Without waiting for a reply he stomped out the door, wincing when an icy ball of snow hit him in the back of the head before sliding under the collar of his coat. He turned around in time to see her gloating smirk just before she slammed the door shut.

It took him a moment to get over the shock—and dig the snow out from around his neck—but then he pictured her adorable face when she thought she'd put one over on him. He grinned. Life with Laurel would never be boring.

Whoa.

Where did that come from? Just because the woman turned him on like a match to a keg of dynamite, didn't mean he needed to think long-term relationship. He bent to gather up the fallen papers and reminded himself how well it turned out the last time he thought with his little head. He'd ended up with a pregnant wife and a truckload of responsibilities.

But Laurel tempted him as he hadn't been tempted in a very long time, and it wasn't only about the attraction, though there was plenty of that between the two of them. He liked that she made him forget his obligations and just be himself for a while when he was with her—without all the excess baggage that comprised his everyday life. It felt good, beyond good. Freeing. Between his daughter, his family, and his job, Jack spent most of his life bogged down by responsibilities. With Laurel everything seemed fresh and new and bright with possibilities. He was loath to walk away from that without giving them an honest shot.

That is if she'd have him.

He knew she wanted him. The feeling was mutual. Her kisses were so addictive. Those expressive brown eyes betrayed her hunger, and her soft hands tugged him closer instead of pushing him away. They made him forget his own name. But he'd made himself a vow after April walked out on him and Tina that he would never let another woman hurt his daughter that way again. And Laurel was leaving soon.

He needed to back away and let her go.

Heart heavy, Jack finished catching up to the slippery pages in the snow, brushed them off, and trudged up the stairs. Laurel must have been watching for him because she opened the door as soon as he reached the top tread. Their eyes met; his were fatalistic, while hers were apprehensive. Jack knew he was on the right track with the case. He just hoped she'd trust him enough to help her.

~~~*~~~

Laurel took one glance at the folder in Jack's hand that she just knew was full of incriminating evidence and felt her stomach drop through her shoes. He was too good a cop not to dig into the background of anyone he deemed suspicious. She'd seen the way he'd looked at Uncle Max and known it was only a matter of time. And speak of the devil.

"Who is it, m'dear?" Max asked from behind her. She stepped aside and a quick frown marred her uncle's brow before he smoothed it out and remarked with forced gaiety, "Sheriff, so good of you to come a
~~~

calling on a chilly night such as this. Laurel, child, hurry and let the poor man in."

Poor man, as if he were a decrepit old guy. Laurel had never seen anyone less frail than the six-four giant ducking his head to enter her home.

"She was just telling me how grateful she is to be under your care… uh, I mean employment," Max said, and slid a sly glance her way.

The crafty old bugger. Trying to weave a sense of responsibility for her onto Jack's shoulders. And was that a glint of humor she saw in Jack's eye? He turned away to close the door before she had a chance to be sure.

"Sheriff, you remember my Uncle Max, I'm sure." She resigned herself to the coming confrontation. Maybe he'd just dropped in for a visit and the papers had nothing to do with them. *Yeah, and pigs fly.*

Jack took his own sweet time to unbutton his jacket and peel it off those mountainous shoulders—she grinned at the residual clumps of snow dampening his collar. He hung it beside her uncle's on the coat rack and brushed a casual hand down his chest to straighten his shirt, tucking the cotton material into his pants where it had worked loose. Her knees quivered in reaction. She licked her lips and bit the inside of her mouth—hard.

"Your niece was just reminding me how cold the snow is, sir." Jack slid a knowing look in her direction before refocusing on the older man. "I'm actually here on business. I have a couple of questions I was hoping you might be able to help me with."

Laurel forced herself to relax, but it was darn hard to keep her gaze off that tan folder.

"We can try, sheriff." Max was all cloying sweetness. Laurel shot daggers in his direction. Did he seriously think Jack couldn't see through his subterfuge?

"I just made a fresh pot of tea and some snacks. Let's go into the den where we can be comfortable, shall we?" As if she could ever get comfortable with the law breathing down their necks. This was a disaster waiting to happen.

Max led the way, with Laurel sandwiched between the two men. Every. Single. Nerve knew Jack followed two steps behind her. The natural sway of her hips suddenly felt like an invitation to have his fingers latch on and pull her back so that she could nestle against his hard… chest. His lips would find her neck and his hands would cover her breasts. They would make love right there, on the floor in front of the fire. Minus Max, of course. Everything within her yearned for things to be different. For her to be a normal woman, free to lo… care for a man like Jack. But she was who she was, and he….

He was the enemy.

Max resumed his seat in the armchair, forcing Laurel to kneel in her previous spot on the floor. She was unwilling to sit next to Jack on the sofa. Not that it mattered; his legs were so long that his knees were still uncomfortably close. She fancied that she could feel the heat of his big body warming her back and his breath tickling her ear. A flush rose up her neck and heated her cheeks. She tried to unobtrusively move away but overbalanced and almost fell into his lap, saving herself at the last moment with a hastily placed hand high on his thigh. His very firm thigh.

The muscles contracted and turned to tempered steel beneath her fingers. She froze. Shocked, she met his amused gaze. Amusement that changed to heated invitation in the blink of an eye. Her tummy tumbled around like a roller coaster ride and she gasped when he placed his hand over hers and gently squeezed.

Oh, my lord.

The back of her fingers brushed against the swelling hardness and she moaned under her breath.

"What's that, my dear?" Her uncle asked.

Laurel jumped and pulled away, but not before she got an eyeful of all… that. Swallowing the sudden dryness in her throat she attempted an easy smile as she turned her back on the temptation behind her.

"Nothing, Uncle. Would you like your tea warmed up?" And if her hands rattled the lid on the ceramic pot a little, hopefully the men put it down to clumsiness.

Determined to get back to a more even footing and find out just how much Jack knew about her uncle, Laurel lobbed the ball into his court.

"So, boss, you going to share what's in that file, or keep us guessing all night?" She passed him a cup of tea made the way he liked it, two sugar, no cream, and was distracted by how carefully he held the delicate English porcelain. The flowery cup looked like a child's play set in his giant hands, yet he handled it with seeming ease.

"Do either of you know a man by the name of Joe London?"

That got her attention.

CHAPTER ELEVEN

The embers in the fireplace spread warmth through Jack's chilled bones. Well, cold except for the spot on his leg branded by Laurel's sweet touch. He glanced around, hoping to see a cushion he could set on his lap to hide his burgeoning arousal. One touch was all it had taken to light a spark that set him burning for more.

Laurel and her uncle were studiously ignoring his question, pretending to doctor up their tea and butter the hell out of a couple of scones. If she stirred one more spoon of sugar into her cup he figured she'd have a nice batch of syrup.

Her fiery locks echoed the color of the fire's flame. It took everything he had to keep his hands in his lap instead of combing them through the silken glory of her hair. He'd never seen anything quite like it, thick and lustrous with kiss-me curls highlighting peaches and cream skin and that little mole high on her cheekbone. She could have made a fortune as a *Victoria Secret* model. *Oh, great*. Now he was picturing her in a sexy little bra and panty ensemble, a set of pearly white wings, and wearing those fuck-me-now red heels she favoured.

Her uncle gave a great hacking cough, jerking Jack's no doubt dazed eyes to meet his back-off-before-I-stab-you-with-this-bread-knife glare.

Laurel reached over and patted his hand. "I told you, you needed to give up your pipe, Uncle. Those things will kill you."

Max smiled at his niece, but kept his gaze glued on Jack. "We all gotta die sometime, ain't that right—sheriff?"

Jack had to give it to the old man. He had balls.

But was he a murderer? That remained to be seen.

"Funny you should mention death, Mr. Doyle." Jack picked up the less than organized, slightly damp file, and passed it to Laurel's outstretched hand. He kept a careful eye on the elder man as she leafed through the top pages. As soon as she reached the mugshot of Joseph Ray London, Laurel slammed the folder shut and glanced back at him, a very real fear darkening her eyes. Jack frowned.

"Something you want to tell me, Laurel?" He silently urged her to come clean. He couldn't help if he didn't know what the hell was happening.

"Laurel," her uncle warned.

She met Max's gaze head-on for a taut moment, then turned back to Jack. "Is he dead?" She held herself stiff and seemed strung as tight as a guitar string, ready to snap at the slightest provocation.

Jack couldn't do it; he refused to be the one to break her spirit. "No. At least we're not sure." Relief flooded her face and she slumped her tense shoulders. She stared at her uncle until Max gave a slight shake of his head. Jack wanted to growl. What were they hiding?

"We found London's car at the Rendezvous Hotel. It was covered in snow, which seems to suggest it sat there since last week's blizzard." He stared pointedly at Laurel, reminding her of their encounter out on the highway east of town.

"Pearl, who runs the hotel, told my deputy that the owner of the Impala had checked in the week before and paid two weeks cash for a room. When he didn't show up to gather his things, she called it in."

Max rubbed his jaw and looked lost without the offensive pipe. He sighed with regret and settled for his teacup, swinging one leg up to rest an ankle on his knee before meeting Jack's gaze. "And what, pray tell, does this have to do with me and the wee lass?"

If they were playing crib the old man just placed him in check.

Jack almost grinned. If the matter weren't so grave, he'd be enjoying this match of wits. Unfortunately, it was serious, possibly dead serious.

"Well, sir, since your daughter—who I believe is currently spending time in a Miami hospital due to a severe beating—lives with the missing person, I figured he might have traveled here to… *visit* you and your charming niece."

Checkmate.

~~~*~~~

Oh, my God, oh, my God, oh, my God. He knows everything.

They were going to jail. And he'd probably throw away the key. Laurel's stomach twisted up so tight a marine couldn't have undone the knots. It was like that time she got food poisoning from eating seafood. Her head pounded as though an entire marching band had taken up residence and her skin felt clammy and yet sweaty at the same time.

This is bad. Sooo bad.

The only chance they had was to come clean. Tell the whole sad story and pray for forgiveness. Any dreams she might have been imagining of her and Jack in a romantic relationship went swirling down the drain.

"We know him," she muttered, "unfortunately."

Max coughed and glared at her before hurrying to correct her words. "What Laurel means, sheriff, is that she and my daughter's… ah, friend, don't always see eye to eye." He took out his napkin and swiped under his eyes, seemingly defeated, though Laurel
~~~

knew better. "You have a wee daughter, don't you, Jack? You must know what it's like having to bite your tongue when she makes mistakes. It's tough being the only parent to any child, but especially a young lady. We want to do right by them and let them live their lives, but protect them from the world at the same time."

He shrugged and took a delicate sip of his tea. The cup rattled against the saucer and he hurried to set it back down.

Even though she knew he was playing the sympathy card, Laurel stretched over the footstool and wrapped her arms around her uncle's neck in a sympathetic hug. She squeezed her eyes closed on the tears and swallowed hard. Max was the only father she really remembered. He'd taken both her and Gabe under his wing and treated them as his own right from the start. And he'd always supported her decisions, whether he agreed with them or not. The least she could do is stand by him now.

She kissed the grizzled cheek so close to her own and leaned back to smile reassuringly into his red-rimmed eyes.

"My uncle is right, Jack. I'm not a huge fan of Bethany's choice in men and I'm afraid I was rather vocal on the subject. But I can't see Joe London driving all this way to try and change my mind." An involuntary shiver slithered down her back at the thought of running into Joe on her own. She didn't know what he was up to—other than embezzlement—but it *was* strange that he would abandon his car.

Unless…

No, what was she thinking? Her uncle would never do anyone bodily harm. Would he?

CHAPTER TWELVE

The next morning dawned crisp and clear, a dazzling winter's day. The Cascade Mountains stood out in stark relief against an impossibly blue skyline, the snow blinding against the brightness of the sun. Before now, Laurel would have set herself firmly in the no-snow-for-me-thank-you-very-much category, but it was hard not to appreciate the sheer beauty of the diamond encrusted snowbanks or the trees wearing lacy snowflake dresses of wedding white. The view from her dining room window was picture-perfect.

She poured a cup of freshly brewed dark roast coffee and opened the newspaper she'd fetched from the doorstep. The newsprint still carried a hint of coolness from the paperboy's sleigh, and Laurel took a deep breath, enjoying the fresh scent. Sunday's were the best; lazy mornings spent in bed, followed by a day of relaxation before the workweek began. She liked to sit and read the news section with the first coffee, then do the crossword after she made herself some multi-grain toast. And if the spot across the table sometimes seemed extra empty, she'd turn on the radio to a good rockin' with the oldies channel, and sing along to dispel the loneliness. Today was one of those days.

She'd just begun her rendition of *"Sweet Caroline"* when the doorbell rang, interrupting her favorite part, the chorus line.

She grabbed her wallet, expecting the paperboy who usually stopped back for his weekly payment after doing the run, but when she opened the door Laurel came nose to whiskers with a bedraggled kitten. Her shocked gaze took in the shivering ball of fur before meeting the worried brown eyes of the girl holding it so gently. Tina.

"Um, good morning?" What was she supposed to say? Laurel had never really spent time around kids.

She liked them; she just didn't know what to do with them. "Cute cat."

"You have to help me… please?" The girl tacked on the request at the last second, pushing her way into the entry. What was it with these Garrett's anyway? "I was helping my friend, Ted Farley, to deliver the papers and we heard this poor little guy crying in the bushes."

Aw.

Laurel's heart turned mushy. The poor thing did look cold. And skinny. How could anyone abandon a defenseless creature that way? She ran a gentle finger over the animal's motley coat and felt the bumps along its vertebrae. It was starving.

"Bring him, or her, into the kitchen and I'll heat a bowl of milk." She waited for the teenager to toe off her boots, then led the way down the hall. Tina sat in the chair Laurel had vacated and hugged the wet fur to her chest, rubbing her nose back and forth over the spot between the kitten's ears. Every now and then a plaintive cry emitted from its throat, as though too weak to do much else. It probably wasn't a good idea to let Tina get so close to the kitten, in case it had fleas or something, but Laurel didn't have the heart to tell her to stop.

She hurried to heat the milk in a small pan on the stove, just until it was lukewarm, and then poured it into a saucer before setting it on the floor.

"Okay, let's see if we can get it to drink a little bit. Who knows when the poor thing ate last?"

Tina gave the critter a last peck on the head then brought it to the bowl and set him down. The kitten wobbled and shook, but never moved from its spot. Tina gave Laurel a worried look, her brows pulled tight over her nose. "What are we going to do now?"

We.

Warmth flooded Laurel's chest. She wasn't used to being needed, at least not without an ulterior motive.

She gave the girl a reassuring look, then crouched down and dunked the kitten's nose in the milk.

"Hey," Tina cried. She attempted to push Laurel aside to save the cat, but Laurel held her off.

"Wait," she urged. "Look."

Sure enough, after a couple spits and sneezes, the kitten realized what he was licking off his fur actually tasted good. He went back to the bowl, dipped his head too far, and got another noseful for his trouble. It took a couple of tries before he finally figured out the trick. After that, he dug right in, on a mission to drink the dish dry.

Laurel looked up into Tina's wide-eyed expression, and had to smile. The will to survive could be a mighty incentive in overcoming adversity. The kid had just learned an important life lesson. If only all traumatic experiences could have the same happy ending.

The kitten started to purr. It was the most pathetically beautiful sound Laurel had ever heard, sort of a cross between a slowly deflating balloon and a blender. She ran a last gentle finger over the boney back, and rose.

"Would you like to wait here while Ted finishes his deliveries?"

Tina eyed her shyly under a mess of nut-brown bangs. Now that the emergency was over, she seemed embarrassed.

"Thanks. I'd like that," she murmured. She shuffled her feet, then stilled when the kitten backed away from the bowl, its belly plump with milk. They watched as he fastidiously cleaned his paws, ears, and chin, then ignoring the girls completely, curled up beside the dish as though scared it would disappear, and promptly fell asleep.

Laurel laughed. Typical male, eat and sleep.

She turned away, leaving Tina to babysit, and went to see if she had any of that scrumptious tasting hot chocolate left in the cupboard. Good, two pouches remained. Laurel filled the kettle with water and turned on the old enamel gas stove. While she waited for the water to boil, she went about setting out a few pastries, cheese, and some blackberries just bought the day before onto a plate and setting them on the table, aware of Tina's eyes following her every move.

"So, you like my dad, huh?"

Laurel froze.

How did she get herself into these kinds of situations? Awkward didn't begin to cover it. What could she say? "Yeah, I love when your dad sticks his tongue down my throat."

Probably, not the right answer.

Feigning a calm she was far from feeling, Laurel turned off the kettle and poured the steaming water over the chocolate mix. She managed to waste a couple more minutes stirring the concoction and searching her cupboard for the last of the dried up mini marshmallows she'd used as a snack the last time she craved sugar.

She carried the two heaped up mugs to the table and tried not to let the fact that Tina was once again in her chair, bother her. Much. There are two things in life that should always be sacred, the remote control for the television, and a person's favourite chair.

Tina's knowing gaze followed her to the other side of the table. "It's okay, lots of women like my dad," she said. "He *is* pretty handsome, for an old guy."

Laurel choked on her drink. *Old guy.* She'd never seen any senior who looked anything like Jack Garrett. His hair was still thick and dark, and while there were a few wrinkles around the edges of his eyes, they were mainly caused by hours of endless squinting into the sun for his job. His body was lean and muscular; while his shoulders were broad enough to protect those he cared about.

Like the girl sitting across from her now, licking the marshmallow off the top of the hot chocolate. A wistful pang of emotion tightened her chest. It must be wonderful to have Jack's unconditional love.

Whoa.

She sat back in stunned shock. Where did that come from? Jack was a great guy, sure, but there were a lot of nice men in the world. It didn't mean she was going to fall in love with all of them.

No, just Jack.

She had. Laurel wasn't sure when, or how it had happened, but she'd gone and fallen in love with the sheriff.

~~~*~~~
~~~

Jack rubbed his ear. Someone was talking about him, at least that's what his mom always said when he complained of a high-pitched whine in the eardrum. She might have been right, or he had an infection. Either way, it was a pain.

He stretched out his body on the leather recliner and then stood up with a groan. He was getting too damn old to be falling asleep in a chair. A glance at his watch showed him he'd slept half the morning away. He shook the cobwebs out and headed down the hall to the washroom.

If his head hadn't been full of all things Laurel Thomas related he might have made it to the bedroom last night. As it was, he'd come home more perplexed than when he left. He'd kept a close eye on Laurel and her uncle when he released the news of the missing man. Neither one knew what had happened to the guy, he was ninety-nine percent sure of it, yet something else was going on. He'd bet his Mustang on it. And how did it all tie into the disappearance of Joe London?

He'd stayed much longer than necessary, and if he was being honest it was because he'd wanted to continue where they'd left off at the front door. The whole night he'd had to fight to keep his hands to himself and concentrate on the reason he'd gone there in the first place, business.

*Yeah, righ*t.

It had nothing to do with the fact that she was on his mind constantly. He couldn't even take a bath without thinking about her. *Oh, hell yeah.* Imagining that voluptuous body plastered next to his in a tub of soapy bubbles was guaran-goddamn-teed to mess with his equilibrium. Now he was going to spend the rest of the day picturing her slippery, wet body in his arms. Good job, Romeo.

He nicked himself with the razor and cursed. Jack needed to get his mind on the job. People counted on him. And he wasn't going to think about what he'd do if it turned out he had to arrest Laurel and her uncle.

CHAPTER THIRTEEN

Laurel spent a surprisingly entertaining morning getting to know Jack's daughter. They had a lot in common; from a love of old-time rock 'n roll, bright colors and fashionable accessories—to Jack.

While they took turns painting each other's nails, one fluorescent pink, the other cherry red, Tina told her about growing up in a single parent household. It was obvious how much she adored her father, even if he did drive her crazy from time to time, especially now that she was old enough to date.

Laurel would have loved to be a fly on the wall the first time some poor kid showed up on their doorstep and was vetted by a glowering Jack Garrett. She could almost hear his warning growl, "Just remember, anything you do to my daughter, I'm going to do to you."

Tina was lucky to have a dad to put the fear of death into her dates. Laurel hadn't been as lucky. A couple of bad episodes had taught her it was safer to keep her distance where the male population was concerned. Until Jack.

Right from the start she'd been attracted to the lawman. His big rangy build and caramel colored eyes softened her from the inside out. He liked to portray a tough guy image, but she'd learned inside was a man who cared deeply for his family and his town. A man who would do anything he had to in order to protect them. Admirable qualities. More than anything Laurel craved a chance to be a part of his life. To care for him the way he cared for others and give him the love he deserved. To be his safe place.

But it could never happen. At least not until she found out what occurred to her cousin's missing ex-boyfriend. Pray God her uncle had nothing to do with it. He'd been acting strange even before Jack dropped that little bombshell. It made her nervous. He wouldn't actually kill anyone—at least she hoped not—but he had some connections that could make Joe's life, shall we say, less than pleasant. Although, if that were the case Max could have made that call from the onset, and saved them all a lot of misery. No, this was something else. She just didn't know what. Yet.

"Do you want me to get that?"

Tina's voice drew Laurel out of her morose thoughts. Her phone sang out her favorite tune of, "Raise a Little Hell" and she smiled. Her brother liked to check on her now and then. After their father died he'd taken on the male responsibilities for their little family, which more often than not ended with him butting heads with Uncle Max. He'd ended up moving out when he turned sixteen, and managed to find a place to stay above a mechanic's garage. The owner took him in, showed him the secrets of the trade, and Gabriel never looked back. But he always remembered to keep in touch with his little sis.

Laurel reached out and hit the speaker button on the phone, careful not to ruin Tina's hard work on her nails.

"Gabe?"

Rough masculine laughter flowed around the room and into her heart. "Still haven't changed my ringtone, huh?"

Laurel grinned at Tina's bemused stare, her hand held mid-motion over the bottle of polish remover. "No, big brother, I think it suits you more now than when I picked it out."

"Ha, ha, very funny. A guy can't get in trouble once with the cops or he never lives it down."

Laurel sent a quick glance across the table, but Tina had slipped away to give her some privacy. Good kid.

"What's up, Gabe?" She hadn't heard from him since he worked on her car before she made the trek up north. Something told her this wasn't a social call though. Her chest tightened. "Is Mom alright?"

Ever since her bout of pneumonia while the kids were still young, Laurel's mom had never quite regained her strength. Throughout their formative years, she'd been in and out of hospitals for various related illnesses. The kids had learned perseverance first-hand. She'd remained positive, no matter what was thrown in their path. Her prognosis? *This too shall pass.* And she'd been right, they'd managed. Sometimes by the skin of their teeth, but they still got by.

"She's good, don't be such a worrywart."

Easy for him to say. No, she took that back. Gabe was almost as bad as Jack for bearing the weight of the world on his shoulders.

"I'm calling about Bethany," he added.

Oh no, he'd heard.

"I think I'd better come up to…what is it, Tipping Stream?"

Tina snorted from her spot beside kitten little, her hand hurrying to cover her mouth as she stared at Laurel with widened eyes.

"It's Tidal Falls, Gabriel, and no, you are not chasing up here to watch over me." She blinked away the moisture clouding her vision, darn allergies. "I'm fine. There's no reason for Joe to come after me, and besides, the police are already looking for him."

For a moment the only sound was the clanking of tools in her brother's garage, then he sighed. "What about Uncle Max?"

Laurel glanced at Tina, and then away, hurrying into speech before he said anything incriminating, "He's fine, I was surprised to see him." She didn't want to lie in front of Jack's daughter, but what choice did she have? They had to continue this charade until Joe was stopped. "He heard of a new treatment in Seattle and decided to stay here while he waits on the results of the tests."

"Tests? What te…"

She rushed to cut him off, "Listen, I have company right now, the *sheriff's* daughter. I'll call later and catch up with the family news, okay?" Her finger hovered over the end call button. "Love you, brother of mine. Take care of yourself, bye." A slight press later and he was gone, leaving a melancholy hole in his wake.

"Your brother sounds nice." Tina said hesitantly. Her earnest gaze searched Laurel's face. "You guys are pretty close, huh?"

Laurel nodded and swiped under her eyes. Yeah, they were. They'd never been the type of siblings who fought over every little thing. Their lives were littered with enough obstacles; they didn't need to add to the drama.

She rose, intending to make a light lunch for the three of them—Ted should be arriving soon. Just then the doorbell rang for the second time that day and Laurel watched Tina's face flare with color, her eyes bright with anticipation. She smiled and waved a hand in the direction of the front hall.

"Can you grab that? I'm going to start lunch." The final words were barely uttered before Tina scrambled to her feet, startling the kitten into snapping awake with a hiss and raised fur. Torn, Tina gazed moved helplessly between the frightened animal and the solid front door.

Laurel let her off the hook. "I'll see to Satan here, you go let Chris in, he must be darn near frozen by now."

Tina took a last look at the spitting mad cat and hurried down the hall. Laurel shook her head. How did she get into these situations? She grabbed a slice of cheddar off the plate and eased closer, hoping to coax the animal into trusting her.

"Okay, you little rodent, it's just me and you. How about cutting me some slack, huh?"

The kitten eyed the hunk of cheese as though it was a T-bone steak and he was a newly minted vegan suffering withdrawals. Wary green eyes watched her every move as Laurel broke off a tiny piece and set it down as close as she dared.

"C'mon, you know you want to," she coaxed, and sure enough, a white-tipped paw with razor claws extended, reached out and hauled the booty in. Happy, now that he'd won the battle, the kitten settled to enjoy his prize, purring contentedly.

"You fraud," she scolded. "You act all tough, but you're actually a sweetheart, aren't you, baby?" She was breaking up the remainder of the cheese when Tina called her from down the hall, her voice a husky plea.

"Laurel, um, can you come here for a minute?"

Laurel frowned. Couldn't she get the door unlocked?

She rose and stepped around the cat before hurrying down the hall, slowing to a halt when she caught sight of what awaited. The cold breeze hit her in the stomach, freezing the fear threatening to choke the breath from her body.

Tina faced Uncle Max in the open doorway, but that wasn't what scared Laurel. It was the nine-millimetre handgun pointed at the teen's head.

CHAPTER FOURTEEN

Jack was too antsy to head into the office, so he called in and took first patrol. The streets were quiet for now, but that would change when Church services came to an end. He tried to attend once a month or so, more for Tina's sake than anything, though he had to admit when those gospel hymns were sung with enough devotion to raise the rafters, even he felt the Spirit.

Between his mom, sisters, Aunt Tess and various nieces, nephews and cousins the Garretts made up a good portion of the congregation.. Even his atheist brother, Ty, had started showing up with his blushing bride, Katy, at his side. Jack never thought he'd say it, but he actually looked forward to those family Sundays. Quite often after church they'd all head over to Ty's house for brunch. Served up potluck style, everyone would bring their favorite dish to share.

The rest of the afternoon would get spent in a variety of ways. Either tag football in the backyard during the warm summer months, or tobogganing in the winter. He knew of a number of families who only came together at weddings and funerals, so he was proud of how close his own were.

The sun was a bright orb glinting off the freshly fallen snow. In his opinion, winter was the most beautiful season of the year. Jack adjusted the polarized lenses on his face. He could easily pass on spring's mud and flooding rivers. Summer's heat, while welcome, made more work in the form of fire watch, especially with the past couple of year's drought—Jack was also a volunteer firefighter—and teenage kids testing out their newfound wings. Fall was nice with its mantle of autumn hues, but nothing compared to Father Winter in Jack's mind. From the lacy perfection of a snowflake, a compliment to the bluer than blue skies, to the majestic Cascade Mountains made him glad to be alive.

So why then, was he so…restless? Pictures of Laurel popped into his mind. Her did-I-just-do-that look when she beaned him with that snowball; decorating the office Christmas tree with Tina while singing off-key carols guaranteed to send any would-be criminals running for cover. He remembered the taste of her lips swollen from his kisses, and her eyes soft with the same overwhelming desire that he could no longer deny.

She tempted him more than any woman had in a very long time. Aunt Tess and Grace had cornered him at the restaurant and warned him not to let her escape.

"You're too good a man to let that bi…" Grace tripped over what she really wanted to say, "bitter woman you married stop you from finding true love."

And when he'd grimaced, Tess had clouted him on the shoulder. "We're serious, you big oaf. Don't waste another minute on the past, the future is staring you in the face, son. Laurel is the real deal, don't let her get away."

He'd be lying to himself if he said April hadn't ripped a hole in his heart when she left. Their affair had been hot and heavy—while it lasted. Unfortunately, she'd only wanted the dream. When reality stepped in and bit her in the ass, first with an unwanted pregnancy and then the loss of his football career, the rosy glow disappeared from her eyes. Jack couldn't afford a loss like that again; it hurt too fricken much. And it wasn't only himself that he had to think about. Tina needed stability in her life. It took her a long time to get over missing her mother. They were a good team, he and his daughter.

But, what if they could make it work with Laurel? Just the thought of waking up every morning with her in his bed was enough to increase his heart rate. She was so vital, a breath of fresh air in his staid world.

He cranked the wheel and headed down the newly plowed street. He needed to see her, talk to her. Then he could get rid of the ache that was making him think crazy thoughts. His hand clenched the wheel. Maybe it was time to take a second chance.

~~~*~~~
~~~

Laurel couldn't draw a breath. Her heart was threatening to jump right out of her chest and join the kitten that had just scurried by and slithered under the straight-backed chair near the door.

She'd seen guns before, of course. *Castle* was one of her favourite television shows, lots of guns there. But it was vastly different seeing one on T.V. and having the muzzle of one pointed at someone you truly cared about. Time slowed. Everything became sharper, clearer, precious.

Why had she waited so long to tell Jack how she felt? She might not ever get a chance now, because there was no way Laurel was going to allow anything to happen to Jack's daughter. Which meant she needed a plan. And fast.

Her uncle looked pale, but composed. A far cry from how she felt at the moment. If this were the mall she'd be pulling the fire alarm and screaming the place down. Unfortunately, there were no bells nearby, and yelling for help would only get one of them shot if the look in her assailant's eyes were anything to go by.

"Where's the cash?" he snarled, his gaze that of an ice-cold killer, or so it seemed in her agitated state of mind.

"My purse is right there—on the table. Take it and leave." Laurel tried to inject a dominant tone into her voice, but it ended in a squeak when he turned the pistol in her direction.

"Do you think I'm fucking around here?" Spittle formed at the corners of his mouth like the rabid dog that he was. "I got nothin' to lose. Either get me the money, now, or I'm going to make you rue the day we ever crossed paths."

Too late.

Tina's teeth were audibly clicking together, but at the same time Laurel caught a glimpse of her father's integrity in her gaze. Please, God, don't let her do something they'd all regret.

Laurel slowly raised her hands in a show of submission, her brain working feverishly to find a way to get them out of this. "Calm down. I'll give you what you want, but the girl gets to leave. That's my deal."

He laughed. The prick.

"Do I look stupid to you?"

Rhetorical question, right?

"The kid stays where she is, that way you're more likely to pay attention. After all, she is your sweetheart's spawn, isn't she?" His grin was demonic.

Laurel shivered. How long had he watched them moving around their daily lives like pawns on a board? Now he was ready to make his move and sweep them all aside in the process.

Unless she stopped him.

"I need time. Do you honestly think I'd keep that kind of money laying around?" She emphasised the money part, hoping to keep the interest focussed on her instead of Tina.

"Look, it's in a safety deposit box downtown. You and I can take a drive and withdraw it from the bank, but if we all go traipsing in there they are going to look at us pretty suspiciously. Is that what you want?" Laurel held her breath and prayed for a miracle.

It came in the form of one half-wild, freaked out kitten. He suddenly emerged out from under the chair and decided to take a run for the open door—between the thief's legs. He must have figured it for a mouse, or worse, because as soon as he saw the animal racing toward him, he screamed like a school girl, threw his hands up in the air and danced a jig worthy of any competition.

"Uncle Max, now," Laurel cried.

Max turned, and seeing his opportunity, leaped for the gun, wrestling with a spazzed out psychopathic idiot, Joe London.

CHAPTER FIFTEEN

Jack rounded the corner of the block and came upon a scene straight out of an episode of *The Twilight Zone*.

What the hell?

A kid, Ted Farley if he wasn't mistaken, stood near an overturned toboggan full of newspapers and was busy rolling them up and hurling them at the trio wrestling?—in Laurel's doorway as fast as any all-star quarterback he'd ever seen.

Her Uncle Max had an arm locked around another man's neck and was yanking for all he was worth, while Laurel pummeled the guy around his head and shoulders.

Jack threw the car into park and had his door open almost before the tires quit rolling. His breath formed little puffy clouds in the crisp air as he raced past Ted with barely a what-the-hell's-going-on glance. The crunch of his booted foot on the snow-encrusted stair turned the focus of attention on him and took away the element of surprise.

Laurel cried out and fell to her knees, the stranger's hand fisted in her hair. Jack growled, adrenaline spiking with his rage. His heart stuttered when he noticed the gun in the man's other hand, and then he saw where it was pointing and his blood turned to ice. Tina stood in the shadows of the entry, tears flowing down her white face. Jack froze, his hands fisting at his side near his own firearm.

Now that he was close enough, Jack recognised the perpetrator from his mug shot. It was their missing man from the hotel.

"Get back," Joe London snarled. "Drop your weapon."

Uncle Max was the first to move, his arms loosening their hold on London's neck and dropping down to his considerably shorter height. Joe straightened and wrenched on Laurel's disheveled mop of hair, yanking her to her feet in front of him.

"I mean it, cop. Move, or I'll blast your little girl to kingdom come."

Laurel's desperate gaze warned him to listen and not do anything rash, but it wasn't easy. Tina's harsh sobs wrung his heart out. What kind of man allowed the women he loved—yes, he knew now without a shadow of a doubt that he was crazy in love with Laurel Thomas—to be placed in danger and not do something about it? Frustration clawing at his insides, Jack did as he'd been told and removed his gun from its holster with two fingers, letting it fall to the snow a few feet away.

"Your niece and I are going for a drive, old man." Joe waved the revolver at Max, urging him to move. The older man shuffled with a stiff gait to Tina's side and wrapped a comforting arm around the teen, then Joe shoved Laurel toward the stairs, his attention split between the two locations.

"Hit the ground," he yelled, his blue eyes almost feverish, his hand clamped around Laurel's forearm.

Jack ignored the command for a moment to stare into her beautiful whiskey-colored eyes in an effort to impart as much strength as he could. She met his gaze valiantly, but her lips quivered giving away her fear.

London squeezed her arm until she winced and let out a whimper. Jack swore, the air around him turning blue. He dropped to his knees and then his chest, hands anchored behind his head. He barely even registered the cold impact of the snow, until he got a close-up of Laurel's feet. The fucker hadn't even let her put on a pair of boots. Instead she was wading through ankle deep tufts in bare freaking feet. Her toes were already turning white from the cold, the red nails almost garish in contrast.

A murderous rage such as he'd never felt before descended. Jack had always taken his oaths seriously, swearing to uphold the letter of the law no matter what the offence. But, dear God, he wanted to kill the man coming down those stairs. Cut him up in little pieces and feed him to the wolves. If he got his hands on him, Jack couldn't guarantee what he'd do.

~~~*~~~
~~~

Laurel hurt. Everywhere.

Joe had taken malicious pleasure in twisting her hair as though he planned on pulling it out, roots and all. Her skin burned from the viselike grip he had on her arm, and her bare feet were froze into hard lumps that made walking almost impossible. But, worse than any physical pain Joe could administer, was the agony of seeing Jack swallow his pride and sink to the ground because of her.

She hated the fact that Jack and Tina were in danger. She'd brought this down on them. Jack would never forgive her and she didn't blame him. All she could do now was get Joe away from them as quickly as possible. The question of the non-existent money would come later.

"You and your uncle thought you were so smart, didn't ya?" He taunted, his breath a stench like rotten eggs near her ear. "Thought you could run away and leave me hanging with that sniveling whelp of a wife while you live high on the hog from all those scams you run. Not this time. Like I explained to your cousin, that kind of dough should be shared with your family."

He pushed her down the first stair and it felt like spikes were being driven into her heels and up her frozen legs. She gasped, and Jack's body jerked as though in pain.

Joe laughed, the bastard.

"It took some persuasion, but she finally came around to my way of thinking and told me where you were. Smart girl."

Not so smart or Bethany would never have come near this jerk in the first place. Laurel kept her focus glued to Jack's dark head. His coat was bunched between his shoulders from having his arms crossed. He seemed almost defenseless laying there on the icy walk. She leaned away from Joe, anxious to put some space between them and Jack, but he only dragged her back.

"Quit horsing around," he warned. "That's how people get hurt." He gave Jack a vicious kick to the ribs.

Laurel screamed. Jack grunted and moved into the blow. He grabbed Joe's ankle and yanked, knocking both Laurel and London to the ground.

Laurel looked up at the blue sky, unable to breathe, but then snow sprayed her face and jerked her back to her surroundings. The air around her was filled with curses and groans as the two men rolled on the ground, each struggling for control over the other. Fists met faces and blood sprayed, coloring the ground beneath their bodies like some kind of abstract painting.

Tina screamed for help, but Laurel couldn't look away from her horrified fascination of the scene being played out in front of her.

The men broke apart and came to their feet with cat-like grace. They crouched, arms akimbo, searching for their opponent's weakness.

Laurel spotted the gun at the same time as Joe. They both made a dive and she landed on the bottom. The air whooshed out of her lungs but her hand was on the weapon. Joe wrapped his arm around her neck and tried to roll her over but Laurel fought him off.

And then he was gone. Seemingly plucked away by a giant's angry hand.

Jack threw him to the ground like yesterday's trash and then straddled the overturned body. He grabbed the other man's arms and yanked them behind his back, ignoring the cry of pain, then reached for his cuffs and clipped them around Joe's wrists. Breathing hard, he leaned back and swiped the blood from his nose.

Laurel stumbled to her feet and lurched across the distance to fall against Jack's broad chest, tears streaming down her face.

Jack fell backward onto his ass and heaved a sigh of relief. It had been touch and go for a minute there. Thank God Laurel was okay. He reached around and pulled her into his arms, careful not to squeeze like he wanted to, so tight that they became fused together. And even then it wouldn't be enough.

When he pictured her diving for that gun and London landing on top of her, his heart stopped. He'd never forget that feeling of utter terror. She'd risked her life for him. He peered down into her tear swollen face and crooked his lips.

"So, that's what you do for entertainment on a Sunday afternoon, huh?"

Her beautiful eyes widened and then slowly filled with humor.

"Wait until you see what I have planned for Monday," she murmured, and met him halfway in a kiss guaranteed to make his world right.

CHAPTER SIXTEEN

Grits and Grace was filled to overflowing with last minute shoppers cramming the small café carrying bags of every color and description. Elvis crooned about a Blue Christmas while excited children pestered their parents and seniors gathered to share fond memories.

Laurel sat in a booth near the back, squeezed between Jack and Tina. Across the table, Jack's brother Ty snuggled with his pretty wife, Katy, while his sisters looked on from their spot at the end of the table. The only ones missing were Jack's parents, who were on their way, and Uncle Max.

After hours of questioning and a promise to reappear for court, Jack let Max go home to his family for the holiday. There would be penalties incurred due to his plot to relieve Grace of her life savings, but Jack's sister who'd agreed to take on the case, assured her it would be minimal. After all, no crime had actually been committed.

Not so for Bethany's ex-husband. Joe was going to get plenty of time to know the inside of a jail cell. Aggravated assault of a police officer is a felony; he wouldn't be bothering any of them for a very long time.

Jack leaned over and peered into Laurel's face. "A penny for them?" he asked, his eyes crinkling at the edges and making her heart go pitter-pat.

She smiled and rubbed her hand along his jean-clad thigh. "I'm just wondering if I remembered everything for dinner tomorrow. This will be my first time cooking a turkey, you know. I hope you have good insurance."

Ty groaned. "Remind me to eat something before we head over," he stage-whispered to his wife.

Katy shook her head and shared an intimate smile with her husband. "That's all you do is eat. You'd think you were the one eating for two."

It took a moment for everyone to comprehend what she'd just revealed. Ty's teasing smile faded, replaced by a look of stunned wonder. His hand reached out and reverently rubbed Katy's still flat tummy, his face filled with awe. She smiled back, her own eyes moist and nodded. "I was waiting until Christmas to tell you, I wanted it to be a surprise."

Ty laughed, elated, and tugged her close. They shared a long, intimate kiss until Jack broke it up with a glance at Tina's rapt look. "Congrats, you two. I can't imagine anyone who deserves a child more than you. Hopefully he or she torments my brother half as much as he plagued me as a kid." He reached across the table and shook Ty's hand.

That comment started a lively discussion on who was the better Garrett child and who got into the most trouble, which they all denied. Laurel sat back and let the conversation flow, simply glad to just be included in this boisterous, loving family in some small way.

The street outside the window was a rainbow of glittering lights. Carollers wandered from store to store spreading their joy of Christmas, and cars cheerfully honked as they drove past, everyone affected by the season.

Laurel hoped Tina would like the gift she'd picked out. Having never bought for a teenager before she'd been nervous of overstepping her bounds, but Jack's Aunt Tess and Grace had assured her it was perfect. She'd gotten the locket engraved and placed a small picture of Tina and one of her dad inside. She'd also enlisted Ted Farley to help find the runaway kitten. He was holding it at his house until tomorrow, his gift to Tina.

Tess and Grace sat at a table across the way, satisfied smiles lighting their grandmotherly faces as they watched the different families. Laurel wondered how many couples they'd had a hand in bringing together and figured the number was high. Their friend, Susan, the cog that kept the restaurant's wheels smoothly turning, joined them. A pair of battery operated Christmas tree earrings flashed in her ears, giving her skin an elfin cast. She set a bowl of soup in front of Grace and pointed. Grace grimaced, but pulled out her kit and took a reading before settling down to eat. Laurel remembered hearing she was recently diagnosed with Diabetes. She was touched by the care in the simple action. These people truly watched out for one another. Small towns were so different from the big cities she'd always lived in.

Suddenly the silence around the table penetrated her thoughts. Laurel swung her gaze around, curious about what she'd missed. Everyone was staring at her. Self-conscious, she looked down to make sure she hadn't popped a button or something, and that's when she saw the box.

It was blue velvet, small and luxurious, and surely at the wrong place setting. Stunned, Laurel looked up and met the solemn, dark-eyed gaze of the man of her dreams.

"Well, you going to open it?" he urged, his unsteady fingers betraying his emotion as he gave it a little nudge in her direction.

Half scared, Laurel reached out and opened the lid as though something might jump out at her. She gasped. Inside lay the most perfectly beautiful diamond solitaire she'd ever seen. Mesmerized, she watched as the stone caught the light from above and refracted into a thousand blue-white rays.

"Wow," she heard someone mutter. Wow, indeed.

Jack's hand under her chin turned her to meet his apprehensive gaze. "Say something."

She would as soon as she found her voice again. He'd managed to stun her into silence, no mean feat.

"If you don't like it, I can take it back," he said, disappointment clouding his expression.

"No," Laurel cried, her voice husky with emotion. "Is this what I think it is?" she whispered.

Now that she hadn't turned him down flat, Jack's face cleared. Eyes glowing, he picked the ring out of the box and slid it onto her trembling hand.

"Laurel Thomas, I'm asking you to be my wife," he said, his tone strong and sure. "To take my hand and share my life. Love me, as I love you. With all my heart and soul. I will protect you to the end of my days on this earth, and beyond. Marry me, Laurel. I'll make sure you never regret it."

Laurel gazed into the eyes of the man who had changed her world and answered the only way she could, "Yes. Yes, I'll marry you. I promise to cherish you, and care for you, and always be by your side. I'd be proud to be your wife, Jack Garrett."

And then she threw herself into his safe arms and burst into tears amid a crowd of cheers.

Reviews are the lifeblood of any successful author. Without you, we can't be heard.

If you enjoy the story, please consider sharing on your favorite social media sites, as well as GoodReads and from wherever you've bought the book.

Thank you,

Jacquie Biggar

Jacquiebiggar.com

OTHER BOOKS AVAILABLE BY THIS AUTHOR

Book #1 in The Wounded hearts Series

TIDAL FALLS

By Jacquie Biggar

Nick Kelley spent the last few years of his life working as a dog handler in the U.S. Marine Corps. His sole focus was to keep his team alive in the midst of chaos. When he fails to notice an IED in time and loses most of his teammates, Nick shuts down. It takes meeting and falling in love with a woman in danger to make him realize life's worth living.

http://jacquiebiggar.com

AMAZON BOOK TRAILER

EXCERPT:

Tracing a slow path up her slender throat, he noticed her pulse fluttering just under her skin. Zeroing in on her plump lips, he groaned under his breath as the pink of her tongue flicked out to moisten them. A banquet for him to savor. Just a little.

"Sara—"

"Look, I'm fine, Jessica can…" She sputtered to a nervous halt as he stepped forward and nudged her legs apart with his hips.

His jeans scraped her bare skin, and he caught the awareness in her expressive eyes. At least he wasn't alone in this. Cradling her hips on the cool countertop, he leaned in, giving her ample time to back away. A few light sips, that's all he needed. His heart pounded so hard it threatened to leave his chest. The plump softness invited him to taste, to feast. His tongue flicked out teasing her, until with a soft sigh, she opened to him. Ravenous now, he sank deep, indulging in the honey and cinnamon taste of her.

Sweet, so sweet.

What was your first memorable kiss like? Sweet? Hot? Somewhere in between?

Subscribe to My mailing list to find out first about upcoming releases, contests, recipes, and more. http://eepurl.com/2MFvX

SECOND IN THE WOUNDED HEARTS SERIES

THE REBEL'S REDEMPTION

By Jacquie Biggar

Annie Campbell has a good life for her and her young son in the mountain town of Tidal Falls. She's dating the sheriff, owns a successful business, and has the support of the community.

So why isn't it quite enough?

Jared Martin left Tidal Falls a hotheaded youth, and now, after eight years in the military, he returns a bitter, disillusioned man.

Then he finds out he's a father.

When an old enemy follows and causes mayhem in the small town, can Jared overcome the odds to protect the woman he's always loved and the child he never knew, or will it be too late?

AMAZON BOOK TRAILER

EXCERPT:

Jared's world narrowed down to the little black barrel of the gun pointed at his chest. Funny, in all the years of being in the SEAL teams he'd never been in this situation. Not to say he hadn't dodged his share of bullets. It's just they'd always erupted like a hailstorm, out of nowhere. This was somewhere. The back alley of his mother's freaking café in freaking America to be exact. *What the hell?*

If he wasn't so pissed off at himself for getting into this situation, he might have laughed. Eight years overseas off and on, and he was going to get shot in his own backyard. How's that for ironic?

"Look man, why don't we talk about this?" Jared forced his gaze to focus on Sergei's steely gaze instead of the muzzle of the semi-automatic.

"The time for talk is past," the Russian said. "You ignored my advice and instead made a fool out of me with that stupid trick you performed."

"Advice? You call beating the livin' shit out of me, advice?" Jared ground his teeth together, and fought to keep a level tone. "You can't blame a guy for wanting to retaliate." A crash by the garbage caused both men to crouch into a fight stance. A tabby cat raced away. Jared straightened, his heart knocking against his ribcage, as desperate to escape this mess as the animal. He needed to defuse the situation before someone came upon them; please God not his mom.

"Okay, you're right. I shouldn't have set off alarms or caused those slots to pay out. But seriously dude, you can't go around acting all KGB, we're in the good old USA now." Jared kept a careful eye on the guy's trigger finger and cursed his loose tongue. What part of defuse couldn't he figure out?

Sergei tipped his felt hat back on his bald head like an old time gunslinger. His hand holding the gun never wavered. "You have big mouth."

Yeah, I've heard that a time or ten.

"Why don't we handle this like two adults? I'll call your boss, tell him I screwed up and it'll never happen again…" There was no doubt on that, if he ever went near a casino again he'd kick his own ass. "And then you can go back to ruling your little kingdom far, far, away."

Click.

The sound of the hammer cocking reverberated with frightening clarity in the small alley. There wasn't even anywhere for him to take cover. The garbage can was at least ten feet away. Jared's jaw cramped from the tension. His skin crawled as if overrun with fire ants. Where was his team when he needed them?

He'd just decided the only alternative was to rush the son-of-a-bitch when the alley erupted with the screams and laughter of children. Two kids rounded the corner at full speed on pedal bikes, racing each other to an imaginary finish line.

Fuck.

Sergei seized the opportunity, stepped between the bicycles and scooped the kids off their seats. The bikes, wheels still turning, fell to the ground in front of him creating a barrier. The kids—God, it was Chris and little Jessica—shrieked until Sergei shook them, then they froze, eyes wide and frightened, hanging under his arms like rag dolls.

"Let them go, you motherfu…" Jared's voice came out low and lethal. Every muscle in his body prepared itself for the moment of attack. His breathing slowed until he could count each heartbeat as the blood coursed through his veins. Waiting. Watching.

Barnikov laughed. Laughed. The prick.

"Now it my turn to play game." Jared made a slight move and Sergei's smile flat-lined. He dropped Jessica to the ground in front of him but kept his forearm wrapped around her neck. The gun nestled the side of her head pointed straight at Chris dangling from his other arm. "Move and I shoot." He shuffled the trio back towards the mouth of the alley. "We'll talk again, my friend."

And then he disappeared around the corner, leaving nothing but the slowly turning tire on a bike and Jared's heart as it shattered.

THIRD IN THE WOUNDED HEARTS SERIES

TWILIGHT'S ENCORE

By Jacquie Biggar

One man's betrayal will seal another's fate.

Ty Garrett fell in love with Katy Fowler from the moment they'd met. When her father's betrayal yanks the young couple apart, Ty becomes bitter.

After a decade away, Katy returns to Tidal Falls with plans to get married in her family's theatre. But she hadn't expected to run into Ty Garrett, the boy she'd never forgotten.

When unseen forces endanger their lives, can Ty save Katy and win back her love, or is it too late for these two star-crossed lovers?

AMAZON BOOK TRAILER

EXCERPT:

Ty muffled a groan. Katy's crooning just about did him in right there. He wasn't sure how Tiger held out, because if she used those words on him in that husky, sexy tone… he wrenched open the back door and dumped the groceries on the floor. A long, deep sigh later he closed the door, placed his hands on Katy's waist and gently moved her aside.

"Here, I'll get her." He climbed into the four-by-four and scooped the recalcitrant kitten into his hand.

"Hey there, Tiger, good job protecting the truck. Come say hi to the pretty lady, and no scratching."

He nuzzled his nose into its soft, furry neck and then passed her down to Katy's waiting hands, their fingers tangling for a too brief moment.

"Hello, beautiful. What are you doing with this guy, huh?" She burrowed her face right into the same spot he had and everything inside him tightened painfully. She was killing him here.

"You find that hard to believe, right?" he grumbled.

She glanced up, her mossy green eyes soft with affection. "What?"

His fingers wrapped around the steering wheel before he did what he craved. Bury his hands in that silken waterfall of hair, drag her close, and see if her neck was half as soft as the cat's. "That anyone would want to stay with me of their own volition?"

Katy frowned. "What are you talking about? I was teasing, Ty. Don't make this into something it's not."

Words to live by.

NOTE FROM AUTHOR

I thought I'd share with you the beginning of my love affair with writing.

Normally, procrastination is my enemy. I like to get done whatever it is, as soon as I can, so that I don't have to worry about it anymore.

In school I worked hard to stay in the top ten every year. So when I came down sick with the measles and missed two weeks of grade nine, I was devastated. How was I ever going to catch up? I had less than a week to write a compelling story for Language Arts or get a failing mark.

Angry and frustrated, I sat in our living room, pen and paper in hand, staring at a bright yellow bouquet of cheerful looking daffodils. I wanted to hurl them across the room. It wasn't fair. Why was I being punished for getting sick?

But then an idea popped into my head. A silly, farcical story. If the teacher wanted an essay, fine, I'd give him one. And so, Count Daffodil, was born. After the first paragraph the words flowed quicker, I could see the scene in my head and needed to get it down on paper. (Sound familiar?) I spent the rest of the day writing, and by the end of the night I had my story.

The next day I turned it in and immediately felt ill all over again. It was dumb. The teacher was going to hate it. I'd be a laughing stock. Funny how easy you can build something up to catastrophic proportions when you lack self-confidence.

We had to wait two weeks for the results. I was on tenterhooks the entire time. Sure that my mom would blow a gasket because I'd goofed instead of giving it my best shot.

Then came the big day.

I was scared to look. Finally, I couldn't take it anymore and turned to the last page. These were my teacher's words:

I'm glad I didn't read this at night. It's been a while since I was so enthralled with a story. Very professionally done. The suspense, the ending, the style was excellent. I think I'll read it to the other classes. Very impressive.

Not only did he read it to the other grade nines, he read it over the intercom to the entire school!

Because of Mr. Thomas and a hapless bouquet of sunny daffodils, a writer was born.

Jacquie's first book, Tidal Falls, a romantic suspense novel about second chances, released September of 2014.

Jacquie Biggar

www.ingramcontent.com/pod-product-compliance
Lightning Source LLC
Chambersburg PA
CBHW061239170626
46809CB00007B/2743

* 9 7 8 1 9 8 8 1 2 6 0 0 5 *